THE SUPERVILLAIN
FIELD MANUAL

Good (Bad) Praise for King Oblivion, Ph.D.,
The Supervillain Handbook, and *The Supervillain Field Manual*

"Without great supervillains, superheroes would have no one to fight but each other! King Oblivion, Ph.D., has performed a noble public service with *The Supervillain Handbook* and deserves the unbounded gratitude of every thinking comic book fan. Excelsior!"

—Stan Lee

"*The Supervillain Field Manual*: For when you've exhausted *The Anarchist Cookbook* and are ready to take the next step."
—Kelly Sue DeConnick, writer of *Captain Marvel* and *Avengers Assemble*

"*The Supervillain Field Manual* is an insightful glimpse into the terrifying genius of King Oblivion, Ph.D. that builds on the groundwork laid in *The Supervillain Handbook*. Credit to Matt D. Wilson for his bravery in risking life and limb yet again to spread the word of the Malevolent Monarch; bequeathing to the reader the hard-earned wisdom of not only *becoming* a supervillain, but *succeeding* as one. [*The Supervillain Field Manual* is] a tome to strike fear in the hearts of the noble, and inspire generations of despots to come!"
—David Marquez, Artist of *Ultimate Spider-Man* and *All-New X-Men*

"*The Supervillain Handbook* offers advice on everything from planning mayhem and crafting dramatically evil rhetoric to recruiting minions and figuring out if you have the right motivation to build toward world destruction. . . . The author knows his stuff."

—*USA Today*

THE SUPERVILLAIN FIELD MANUAL

How to Conquer (Super) Friends and Incinerate People

**King Oblivion, Ph.D.
(as told to Matt D. Wilson)**
Illustrated by Adam Wallenta

Skyhorse Publishing

Skyhorse Publishing books may be purchased in bulk at special discounts for
sales promotion, corporate gifts, fund-raising, or educational purposes. Special
editions can also be created to specifications. For details, contact the Special Sales
Department, Skyhorse Publishing, 307 West 36th Street, 11th Floor, New York,
NY 10018 or info@skyhorsepublishing.com.

Skyhorse® and Skyhorse Publishing® are registered trademarks of Skyhorse
Publishing, Inc.®, a Delaware corporation.

Visit our website at www.skyhorsepublishing.com.

10 9 8 7 6 5 4 3 2 1

Library of Congress Cataloging-in-Publication Data

The supervillain field manual : how to conquer (super) friends and incinerate
people / King Oblivion, Ph.D. (as told to Matt D. Wilson) ; illustrated by Adam
Wallenta.
     pages cm
  ISBN 978-1-62087-633-6 (pbk. : alk. paper) 1. Criminals--Humor. 2. Comic
books, strips, etc. I. Wilson, Matt D. II. Wallenta, Adam illustrator.
  PN6231.C73S86 2013
  818'.602--dc23
                          2013002973

Printed in China

For Pud, of the Phantoms

You're too late, you ignorant whelp! This book has already put you on the path to your end!

You hesitate to act. As you read these words, as your eyes dart from sentence to sentence, you feel . . . an intrusion. A burning sensation in the back of your neck. You choose to ignore it. You chalk it up to hypochondria. The feeling spreads upward into your brain and down through your spine. You begin to consider whether something has bitten you. Perhaps a spider stuck in your underwear? The feeling is too real to be psychosomatic. Something, someone, somewhere is causing this ever-growing pain, taking over your frail, feeble body.

You try to stand. It's impossible. You reach for your phone to call for help, but your arm refuses to heed your command. Your body is no longer yours. You cannot control it.

Because I do.

Mwa-ha-ha! I'm just messing with ya. You can move. Go ahead, wiggle around, I'll wait.

See? You're fine. If you're not, I didn't have anything to do with it, and my lawyer, Intimidatrix, Esq., can attest to that.

In my previous book, *The Supervillain Handbook*, which I assume you read, because you're probably one of the thousands of poor souls I forced to read it at that old abandoned sawmill, I explained all the ins and outs of making a name for yourself in professional supervillainy. What you may not have realized when you finished that tome was that ending did not represent the end of the story; that is, your story of professional super-evil. Stories aren't just beginnings . . . they have middles and ends. And though it seems like it's only the beginners who need guidance, everyone who isn't as naturally and awe-inspiringly dominant as I am occasionally needs a push one way or another, at all stages of his or her career.

So here we are. You, me, and this guide: *The Supervillain Field Manual*. In these pages, you'll learn the skills of finer manipulation, not unlike what I did to you in those opening paragraphs, you gullible, gullible, tadpole of a human being. You'll come to understand that not all supervillainous acts are physically destructive ones, though that's just as important. You can do just as much bad through public relations as you can with an industrial disintegrator (if you have any experience in PR, you already know this). You'll learn that it's simply not always possible for you to accomplish all your goals on your own (again, unless you're me). You'll learn that people you work with quickly become deadweight and need to be cut loose. And you'll learn that, eventually, the time will come to hang up your tights or metal onesie or invisibility hat or whatever it is you wear.* You'll also become aware that anything having to do with supervillains and superheroes, regardless of quality, will always, always get a sequel.

---

* Important Note: The day I retire is the day I take everyone else with me. Remember that.

Are you ready? It's time to go from beginner's badguy-ism to advanced evildeedsery.

Let's make this happen, if you can manage to turn the page.

This is Max Badguy. Remember him? Not many people do. That's why he needs this book.

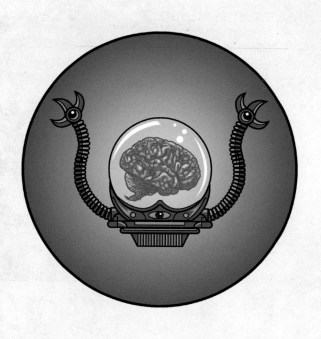

CONTENTS

Prologue

A Quick Recap (Before
I Break Your Kneecaps)

As I mentioned earlier, this is the second book in a progression of definitive (you can call them sacred if you'd like) instructional texts regarding the profession of supervillainy. If, for some reason, you didn't read the section before this, maybe because you have some weird, infuriating habit of reading things out of order or you hate sections of books that don't have headings—supervillains often have weird tics, so I've seen them all*—that book is called *The Supervillain Handbook*. If, for some even less comprehensible reason, you didn't read *The Supervillain Handbook,* allow me to shatter your kneecaps with my Telekinetic Gaze (I'm working on a trademark on KinetiGaze) after I provide you with a quick rundown of what you missed.

Bear in mind that this summary should in no way serve as a substitute for reading *The Supervillain Handbook* in its entirety. You certainly don't want to find yourself staring down the hammering fist of your local superhero or worse yet, the barrel of the death ray of a rival supervillain. The worst is finding yourself in a situation akin to only having skimmed the CliffsNotes for *The Great Gatsby* the night before you had to recite every word to the ghost of F. Scott

---

* Though that doesn't mean I tolerate them.

Fitzgerald himself, nude.* (I know a guy this happened to once, and Fitzgerald's ghost was terribly unforgiving.)

HELP...ME...

But since we're here now and it would probably be *so difficult* for you to put this book down and go buy another one on your tablet—by the way, we're working on our own, new, exciting version of a tablet that gradually and permanently attaches itself to people's hands and, over a few months, turns them into tablet people we then re-sell as tablets, which is pretty exciting—we'll run you through the basics so you can continue:

- Supervillains can be motivated by lots of things, but *theatricality* is the thing that truly separates the supervillain from the everyday jerk.
- **Advanced degrees** or **titles of nobility** are the most effective doorways to instant supervillain status, though it's also effective to kill an important person and assume his/her identity.
- There are plenty of (in)appropriate goals for a supervillain to have: greed, bloodlust, power-madness, getting your rocks off, just plain being bat shit crazy—but the most important thing is knowing what will ultimately satisfy your hungry soul.
- Choose a persona, nemesis, and costume for yourself that fits your MO, your skill set, and your name.
- **Never stop talking.**

---

* This is not meant as an insinuation that *The Supervillain Handbook* is a comparable work to *The Great Gatsby*. I think we all know how far, far, superior the former is as a work of literature.

- Superpowers are important, but they're not everything. You can supplement or replace powers with technology. Whatever you get, you're likely going to have to pay for it.
- Henchmen are idiots, but you have to hire them for two key reasons:

  First, you need cannon fodder to throw toward rampaging superheroes with reckless abandon.

  Second, they're unionized.
- You've got to lay your head somewhere. It's preferable that place also have a giant throne made of skulls and an escape hatch.
- The grander your evil schemes and dastardly plans, the more likely you are to make a mark.
- You will get punched in the face. You will go to jail. You will die and come back to life . . . probably multiple times. These come with the job. Deal with it.

Short of me reducing every glossary definition and timeline entry down to a few letters, that's a pretty thorough summary. I guess one other thing I should mention is that I used a machine called the Psychomonitor to steal every reader's thoughts, and now I remotely control all their minds; but that's merely a minor detail. Forget I even said anything!

That was a pretty valuable start, if I do say so myself (and I do; don't you dare question my judgment either, lest you find yourself bedazzled as a human jewel on my celebratory sparkle jacket), but you have so much more to learn. Last time around, I didn't even get into how much of professional supervillainy is PR. You've got to be able to handle that shizz.

So let's get down to it.

THE SUPERVILLAIN
FIELD MANUAL

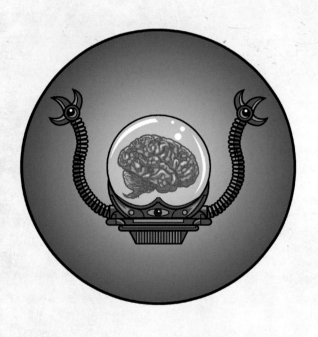

Chapter 1

Announcing Yourself

A lot of supervillains make one major mistake at the start of their careers: They think filling a bank full of purple gas to knock all the patrons out, then removing the vault by chaining it to a helicopter, then opening the vault by pouring acid on it, and finally draining that acid onto the city charter is enough of an event to get people to notice them. They think it'll force people to learn their name. And, true enough, a stunt like that will get you *some* attention. You'll get on the news; hell, they might even show your picture on there and an anchor may say your name a few times. But consider that the name they're going to say is most likely going to be the one you were born with, not the one you took a lot of time and care coming up with (assuming it's not 'The Gasser' or 'Vault Absconder' or something similarly half-assed). Why is that? Because you *didn't even bother to say it out loud, you **closed-lipped imbecile***! Also, nobody really watches the news anymore. Maybe your grandma, but odds are she made the costume for you* and none of this is going to be news to her.

---

* Lots of supervillains get their start this way; in the days before they are able to pull together the money for some grade-A equipment. There's no shame in it, though you should be aware that if I see you in a grandma-made outfit, I will shame the ever-living hell out of you.

There's an old saying, most likely coined by an idiot, quite possibly a superhero, which states that actions speak louder than words. I suppose actions say *something*, in that they technically say, "Hey, look at this thing I'm doing!" But it's up to you to give those actions context. If you got anything at all from the previous book—and if you didn't, what compelled you to read this one, a love of not fully comprehending wisdom?—it should have been the notion that the key to any effective supervillain act is making it a show. A spectacle. Something dramatic. Melodramatic, even. If you learn anything from this one, it's this: **People need to know your name.** And they can't know it if you don't tell them what it is.

Let's take it even one step further. Your name shouldn't just be one that people can identify when they hear it. You need to go beyond simply being a household name; you have to become an insomniac's name, to coin a term.

Here's what I mean: People in your neighborhood, your city, within a 200-mile radius or so, should stay awake at night wondering what you're up to. "I wonder who he's transforming into gelatin?" they might lie on their rock-hard mattresses thinking at 3:00 a.m. Or they'll consider, "Has she shrunk to the size of a ladybug? Is she inside my safe, stealing all my bearer bonds right now?" in the dead of night while trying to grab some Z's on the couch because they're so scared to find that their waterbed is full of ladybugs again.*

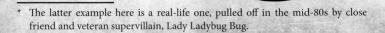

MAX BADGUY IS GOING TO KILL ME!

* The latter example here is a real-life one, pulled off in the mid-80s by close friend and veteran supervillain, Lady Ladybug Bug.

Supervillain FAQ: What should I do with my hair?

Whether it's the wavy craziness or Norman Osborn's Brillo pad, the semi-sentient grip-strength of Medusa's locks or the electric intensity of Livewire's shock, the way you wear your hair says something about who you are. That's especially true if you're a supervillain, and you need everybody to know what your deal is the second they first set eyes on you.

But which hairstyle works best for you? Consider these basic styles and customize to your liking:

High and Tight
If your shtick is some kind of pseudo-military, authoritative yell-casting, a nice buzz cut would be perfect.

Bowl Cut
Reserved strictly for Doctor Octopus. Sorry.

Unreasonably, Unmanageably Long
Enjoy your twelve hours of shampooing, lady villains!

Bald
It's fine to Luthor it up. Go Luthor on 'em! That goes for you too, ladies, after you get sick of having all that hair.

Ponytail
Perfect if your villainous persona is "douche."

Wild and Unkempt
Do you think of yourself as a feral beast, unable to control your wild urges? Do you have fangs? Is someone having to read this to you because you're too busy tearing into an antelope? If so, then this is a good choice for you.

Pronounced Spikes
You know, these might look terrific, but pretty much whatever you do, you're going to be mistaken for a Dragonball guy. You don't want to be mistaken for a Dragonball guy.

Mohawk
Perfect for punkish-thug-type supervillains. This is especially true if you're some kind of animal-human hybrid and you need to prove that you still know the streets.

One of those Monk Cuts with the Bald Spot
It would certainly be surprising.

Cornrows
You know, I haven't really seen it that much, but why not? I'd think someone could pull it off.

Green
Hard to go wrong with green. Doesn't much matter what you do with it if it's green.

An Incomprehensible Optical Illusion
Terrific if you need a distraction so you can escape from superheroes without having to bother with a fight.**

Helmet that You Never Take Off
Not actually hair, but you don't need to worry about your hair if no one ever sees it. And who knows? Maybe you burned the helmet to your head and it doesn't come off anymore. Perhaps you could style the helmet to look like hair for special occasions.

Sentient
Having hair that does your bidding is downright awesome, but you have to be careful. It can rebel, and there's nothing quite as obnoxious as trying to put down a pesky

---

** This is called Osborn-style.

nuisance that is made of hundreds of thousands of individual strands.

All over Your Body
Are you a gorilla? This is your only real choice. If you are not a gorilla, I'd advise against it.

So how do you broadcast yourself, your name, your actions, your face, your laugh, a ton of hypnotic spiral-patterns, so pervasively into people's lives? You have a few options, all of which you may want to take advantage of. The more you get yourself out there, the more sleepless nights you'll be causing.

Write an Open Letter

In the old days, back when I was getting into the supervillainy game, there was a very clear, very well-established process for letting everyone know who you were and that you were ready to shoot some monuments into space. What you did was write a letter to your local newspaper, maybe in your own handwriting or possibly in cut-out letters from a magazine. It didn't really matter how you wrote it, because you'd be signing it anyway. After all, you'd be getting your name out there. For some added flair, you'd tied it to something—like a brick or a time bomb or a city councilman's mustache—and have a shadowy henchperson drop it off at the front desk.

The letter would always include some sort of threat, like: "If you don't print this in tomorrow's paper, I'll start taking everyone's mustache. No mustache will remain on any lip!" Men in power loved their mustaches back then, so the editors would print the letter just like clockwork. And just like that, you'd be an overnight sensation. Quite literally, in one night, you'd have everyone in the city talking about you while taking out facial-hair insurance policies or closing their for-certain-doomed men's groomeries.

Obviously, things don't work like that anymore. People nowadays are quite cavalier about their facial hair. Also, most don't really read newspapers, like they don't watch the news. They just get update chimes on their smartphones (and there's got to be a takeover plan for that somewhere), but that doesn't mean an open letter won't work anymore. You just have to send it to more places than before. Start with all your local news websites, maybe some places that cover local sports or needlepoint or foot fetish porn. People live in their own little worlds now. And while you're at it, post it to some forums. Get a Tumblr. Draw up some *Sonic the Hedgehog* fan art to attract a horde of followers, and then hit them up with the letter.

Of course, the threat has to be updated, too. People love their tattoos. Maybe tell everyone you'll steal their tattoos and replace them with your name. Actually, that's pretty clever. And that gets your name out there in another way! You guys, I am pretty smart.*

---

* You can agree. You *must* agree.

Write Your Name Somewhere Visible to Everyone

Remember that scenario I was talking about a minute or two ago; the one where you were going to steal the bank vault with a helicopter and then open it with acid? That plan would go from a dud to a stud with one simple change: Instead of dripping the acid all over some colonial, founding city document, pour it out on the city's main public square and spell out your name. Bam! You just put a huge, melty period on a heist well done.

Of course, it doesn't have to be acid or the public square. Skywrite it if you're into gimmicky stuff like that. You could also take over the city's power grid and light up every building so that they spell out your name, and maybe add a quick message about how today you own their electricity, but tomorrow you'll have access to the switch that controls their very lives. That's got a nice ring to it. If you want to get really creative, seize the Chef Boyardee® soup factory—a pretty sweet spot for a hideout, anyway—and make it so the only pasta letters it produces are the ones in your name. It's a little more cryptic than some might prefer, but you can't help but admire* the moxie it would take.

The one place you probably want to avoid melting or drilling or carving your name into would be the moon. It would certainly be a visible place to stick your moniker, but I mean, come on, it's been done . . . to death. (Literally. I know a guy who died up there trying to blast his name into

---

* Don't take this as some sort of guarantee that I will admire you if you manage to pull any of this stuff off. Odds are I will never admire you. It's nothing personal, but compared to me, you're trash. Understood?

a crater. He was a wild guy. Remind me to tell you about him if I ever meet you in person, which I won't.)

Relay Your Message through a Superhero

Superheroes are documented blabbermouths. They can't help but chatter about who they've fought recently and how much good they're doing for the world and blah blah blah. That galling habit is something you can use to your advantage.

Plan one of your early devious exploits so that it will attract the attention of a superhero. One way to guarantee that one of these fools will show up is to put his or her significant other in imminent danger or threaten the bus the hero's great aunt rides home every afternoon. It's really easy to make that happen if you have a local superhero with a well-known "secret" identity, as many of them do.* If somehow the superhero of your choice has been cautious enough to keep their true identity a secret, just cause a little bit of mayhem at say, a parade. Someone the superhero loves is bound to be there, and the Law of Coincidences† dictates that the superhero will, too.

Then, during your fight, the superhero is pretty likely to ask, "Who are you anyway?" That's when you tell them, "Let the world know that I am _____!" They'll do it. They'll do anything you say. They're so gullible. (They'll probably hit you a lot too, so just be aware of that.)

---

* Seriously, superheroes are basically terrible at keeping their masks on.
† Anything that can happen to facilitate a superhero/supervillain fight will happen, no matter how unlikely or improbable.

Leave a Calling Card

Following your first few heists, kidnappings, rampages, or whatever you opt to do, you may want to consider dropping something at the scene to clue the local authorities and/or superheroes that you're a force to be reckoned with. That something could be a literal card. Seriously! It could be just a regular old business card or maybe a piece of paper that's been dipped in some sort of psychotropic substance and makes whoever touches it think about nothing but you and how terrifying you are for a few hours. That would be rather effective.

That said, lots of things could be used as calling cards. It's a bit of a cliché, but it's pretty fun to leave behind cryptic clues leading to your next master crime in the form of riddles, puzzle boxes, or childlike crayon drawings. For this to work, it's pretty important that you make sure the investigators who are going to be picking this stuff up aren't complete dolts. Otherwise, they won't notice or they'll think a kid who loves word-finders showed up and made a bunch of marks on the wall right after someone stole all the billion-dollar art paintings with ultra-rare liquid rubies. They also have to be willing to play along in your cat-and-mouse game. Some investigators look for and find real evidence—like DNA and whatnot—and ignore the cryptic clues. Avoid those people if this is what you're going to go for.

If you're a particularly sadistic individual or your power is that you can regenerate your body parts, you could also leave behind a limb or two. If they're your own, the forensics experts will test the DNA and find you (though, again, they'll probably only be able to dig up your birth name).

If they're someone else's, you're going to have to thumbtack a note to them or something. You know what? The smart thing would be to do things the easy way and use some Post-its™, no matter whose body parts they are.

WORST PRACTICE IN ACTION:
Dr. Doom Introduces Himself

In his first encounter with the meddlesome freaks in the Fantastic Four, supervillain master Victor Von Doom threw a net over the team's headquarters at the Baxter Building, took the Invisible Woman hostage, and sent the other three back to Blackbeard times. That's a terrific, Byzantine, and crazy opening plan, but the true beauty is how quickly he was able to make an impression. The net, along with the loudspeaker announcement of his arrival, clued old college rival, Mr. Fantastic, into who Doom was immediately.

Teaching Moment: Choosing an arch nemesis who was an old friend and/or competitor during your younger days means you can use automatic shorthand when introducing yourself. All you have to do is make sure your old college roommate becomes a superhero. Throw him or her into some chemicals to try to make this happen.

Take over a Broadcast Station

As I noted before, radio and television don't have the universal pull they once did, but that doesn't mean it isn't worthwhile to use those media outlets to your advantage. People still watch tons of garbage, after all. Why not make it your garbage?

Here's a clever way to go about it: During one of your early capers, have your henchmen infiltrate a local TV or radio station, incapacitating the crew—they often work on shoestrings anyway—and get to the control room. Then have them play a pre-made tape of you narrating exactly what you're doing on the job as its happening. It'll be so theatrical that people won't even know how to contain themselves! Just be careful to make your gleeful discussion about the monster you're attacking the city with or whatever is you're doing vague enough that the authorities don't step right out of the police stations and hero caves to find you instantaneously; make sure to find a good hiding place. Along those same lines, don't record the video at a recognizable place, like, say, your aunt's house. They'll know it was your aunt's house.

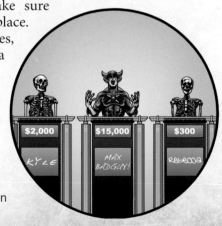

Nationally syndicated TV programs can get you even wider attention.

You might be thinking right now,* "This is the twenty-first century. Rather than taking over some stodgy old TV station tower or satellite, why not put this selfsame video on YouTube and let people watch it there?" Here's why not: Because YouTube isn't live, you pus bucket. You can't just let people watch your as-it-happens account of your villainous exploits whenever they want. Upload it to YouTube afterward, sure, but the real deal has to air live.†

Force Someone to Write a Song or Make a Film About You

Up-and-coming bands and aspiring filmmakers are always looking for their big break. Give them one! Threaten to break their pelvis if they don't immortalize you and your evil, evil deeds in a song or film. People eat that kind of shit right up, and, who knows, they may even admire you because you were in a movie. Pick whatever genre you want: horror, black metal, action, hip-hop, romantic comedy, K-pop. It doesn't matter, as long as people see or hear it.

Of course, the more experienced and popular the musician and directors are, the more likely they'll be to have some traction. . . . Just remember that it'll to be a lot harder to kidnap Steven Spielberg or Coldplay out of their beds, since I already have them here with me.

---

* Of course you are. I know you are. I own your thoughts, remember?
† Any more questions like that, and I'll be uploading you to YouTube . . . in one of those cat videos. You'll be the box the cat tries to jump into. Trust me, I can make this happen.

Brainwash Everyone into Believing You are the Greatest Possible Threat to Their Safety

If you can take over a satellite, which we already discussed above, this shouldn't be too terribly difficult for you to pull off.

Whatever you choose to do, remember: Get your name out there. The important name; your supervillain one. How people address you and whether they know you at all will make all the difference when it comes to determining whether you can build a reputation as a true supervillain or end up being just some weirdo jerk.

A Semi-Legitimate Method: Mastering the Art of the Interview

All the techniques for putting your name of the tip of everyone's tongue listed elsewhere in this chapter are . . . well . . . you might call them rather, forward. Forceful, even. I tend to think that supervillians should be aggressive when it comes to making one's mark with that ever-important opening statement. However, not all supervillains can come out of the gate at quite the full gallop. Some, for the sake of their all-important plans, must give the world the initial impression that they are legitimate businessmen (more on this in Chapter 12), or at least, not complete psychopaths. Those types can't go seizing radio stations or rearranging highways to spell out a message of contempt for everyone else.

No, those supervillains have to go for a more traditional way of making themselves known. . . . A method that can go awry easily and without warning. That's right, they have to do media interviews. How does one maintain his or her evil credibility while also presenting a law-abiding veneer? It's not easy, but it's doable. Follow these guidelines and you might pull it off.

1. Smile

Just keep smiling. Smile the whole time. Even if it's a radio interview. The listeners will hear the smile in your voice. Some people might think your smile is creepy, but that's better than them seeing a scowl or a grimace and looking into the very heart of hatred. Do try to normal-up your smile as much as possible, though. Don't lean your head forward and do one of those Jack Nicholson, *Shining* smiles. Actually, that's a pretty useful rule of thumb in general, if you want to look not-evil. Don't look like Jack Nicholson in *The Shining*.

2. Wear Nice, Non-Supervillain Clothes

Cloaks, masks, and goggles don't go over so well on TV. Stick with a nice business suit. (Some villains actually wear suits as their costumes, which is fine. This will be easy for them.) Maybe a casual skirt or khakis. You can change right after. Try not to fidget. You have to look like these clothes are something you'd want to wear for some godforsaken reason.

3. Deny

Deny everything. "According to sources," the interviewer might start, "your company's factories are making members of your very own board of directors into gargoyles!" Or maybe they'll ask something like, "Any truth to the rumors that you're working with a robot from space bent on the enslavement of most of humanity?" Respond with, "I'm not sure what you're talking about. I've never heard this word, 'gargoyles,'" or, "You must have your facts wrong. There is no such thing as robots. Or for that matter, space."

4. Talk up Your Charity Work

You don't actually have to do any. You should start your own front-charity to launder your money through (more on this in Chapter 12 also), however, and constantly mention how much work you do with it in the interview. In fact, start every sentence like this: "With my charity work, my favorite type of coffee is iced," or, "With my charity work, I don't know the first thing about how the city's water got turned into catnip."

5. Avoid Threatening to Kill Anyone

I know, I know. This is extremely unfair. But these people often take this stuff really seriously, and vowing excruciating death for your arch-nemesis usually gets them all flustered.

6. Avoid Killing Anyone

Same deal. Interviewers go nuts and completely freak out about this like it's a big deal.

7. Make Sure Your Henchmen Are Far Away

They are going to completely botch everything right up if they are even in the same building. Send the dumb shits to Dave & Busters® or wherever it is they like to go.

Chapter 2

When You Lose

Listen, I'm going to tell you something you're probably not going to want to hear right now. You should definitely sit down for this. If you're reading this on a treadmill or an elliptical machine, just sit right down on the apparatus. You need to sit down that badly.

Okay, here it is: I have said previously, on more than one occasion, that my supervillain organization, the International Society of Supervillains, had all but wiped superheroes off the face of the planet. That was a lie;* a half-truth, anyway. The truth—and savor this, because you're not going to get this out of me very often†—is that there are lots of superheroes out there in the world; probably one or more in every city . . . some even in small little towns. Seriously, they're like insects.

What we have done is clearly and forcefully broken the back of the organization known as the League of Right Rightness, largely neutralizing the superhero network that grew to power during the twentieth century. Even with that all-important work done, thousands of independent vigilantes with notions that they somehow know better than the rest of us what's "right" and how to uphold the law try every day to get all up in our business.

---

* You're not really *that* shocked, are you? Consider the source, folks.
† And if you try, I'll booby trap my brain to explode if you try to extract any more truth out of it.

Max didn't get away in time.

And while you're sitting down, I'll offer another little tidbit you're probably not going to like: A lot of times, those meddling muscle people, with their big smiles and hair arranged into letters, well . . . they win. Not because they're superior—anything but! It's because they have it easier. Think about it. You spend months, maybe years, crafting a scheme that requires every single little thing to go exactly as you planned. You choreograph and you orchestrate, you ensure your machinations run like clockwork. It's extremely tough and time consuming. And what do they do? They see on the news that you sabotaged a local utility, fly out the window to your location, and hit you until you can't stand up anymore.

How is that fair? They're always on offense, but it's not like you're just playing defense. You're on defense, you're playing offense, you're coaching, you're building the arena, you're the entire grounds crew, and also have to make sure that you cover the spread. To mix a few metaphors, the deck is stacked against you.

Supervillain FAQ: Should I be a mentor?

Everyone reaches a point in their career where they wonder if it isn't time to start sharing the gifts of their wisdom with the younger and less experienced practitioners of their profession.* And while that inclination is awfully noble—which therefore makes it reprehensible—it's also astonishingly egotistical, and I can definitely get behind that.

That's why I took the route of writing these instructional books to rise the tide and therefore all the ships within supervillainy.** Others don't have the ability to threaten the families of *every* employee at a New York publishing house with poison, though, and have to settle for just teaching all their tricks to one lucky student.

* You're welcome, *everyone*.
** Important Note: If you don't have a ship, get one.

But who should your mentee be? Look to these criteria:

It must be someone you trust with every fiber of your being.
To be perfectly clear, this is probably no one.

It has to be someone who will not double-cross you.
Again, this is problematic, given that you'll be teaching them important double-crossing techniques.

Will this person try to kill you and take over your criminal empire?
If you're any kind of teacher, then almost certainly.

In the event this person can somehow be trusted and won't double-cross or kill you, you have to ensure they won't do idiotic things, like reveal your true identity to all your henchmen or enemies.
This a long shot.

If, somehow, this person meets all these criteria, you also have to keep them from naturally usurping you by simply becoming better than you at evil.
And look, they're young, and you're not getting any younger. It's inevitable.

Long story short, don't bother with mentoring. That's what I'm saying.

Here's the capper: Because you're the bad guy—at least in the eyes of the public—you'll get no recognition for any of your effort. You'll be derided as a loser and a scoundrel* who got what they deserved. Forces in the hero-loving world are going to try to shame you into obscurity or recontextualize you so that you're a joke rather than a threat.

Don't let them!

Don't allow them to pressure you into giving up!

Work smart, spin things to your advantage, and you'll maintain your aura of ominousness.

The Preparation

Superheroes get a ton of credit for being prepared; for being able to slip through the noose when we villains cash in on our grudges and push ahead with our Byzantine revenge plots. But look, a lot of that is merely luck. Superheroes are lucky, lucky bastards. Like when it turns out that they have just the right enzyme to cut through the very specific, super-strong cellulose their enemy made the ropes out of. Or they studied up on mutant alligators and learned a song that can put them to sleep in seconds. How is that anything but coincidental?

The answer is that it isn't. Coincidence and Fate may be a supervillain's worst enemy. I have a theory that those two are living beings that actively work against us. This is yet another reason why we shouldn't get anything close to the bad rap we get when it comes to our "loser" status, and should perhaps declare some kind of attack on Coincidence and Fate, but I digress.

Back to my point: You have to be ready for luck to bite you right in your becloaked ass. Otherwise, you'll go to

---

* In less-informed circles, this word has a sadly unfavorable connotation.

jail—or maybe death—looking quite the fool. So before you make a move against the one you're sworn to hate, be sure to have these things in place first:

An Escape Route

Whether it's a jetpack, some sort of helicopter contraption on your back, a drill that creates underground tunnels, a teleportation machine, or having some guys in an idling car nearby so that you can jump in, it is imperative that you enter into any potential conflict or melee with an exit strategy. And since virtually any situation could potentially become a conflict or melee, that means you should have an exit strategy for every potential circumstance, even if you're just sitting at home watching reruns of *Breaking Bad*. Have that drop chute ready to go. (But try not to mistake any loud noises from fictional meth-related crimes for an attack on your HQ.)*

Henchmen

You can buy yourself a precious minute or two by throwing a handful—or if you have the resources, a battalion—of henchmen at your opponent(s). That minute could mean the difference between you being in a brig somewhere or waiting around in a Global Brotherhood of Minions regional post to grease some wheels and wait for new recruits.

Decoys
Mannequins?

Those might fool someone with no superpowers what so ever for a second or two (and they're pretty creepy, so that's a bonus).

---

* More about planning specific exit strategies in Chapter 11.

Holograms?

Cool, but as soon as a superhero swings a punch at one, they know they're hitting nothing but light. Actually, that's probably giving them too much intellectual credit, but they know they're not hitting you in the face.

People in Disguise?

Fine, until someone gets close enough to see their faces or hear their voices—and for some superheroes, they can make such distinctions from a city away.

Clones?

They're awful and melt easily.

Your Best Bet?

Robots that look exactly like you. Sure, they're pretty expensive, and you can bank on at least one getting destroyed every few days or so, but it's so, so worth it. Plus there's the added bonus of sending them to social functions and stuff you don't want to attend. That's right, Aunt Penny, that wasn't me at your fourth wedding! Mwa-ha-ha!

Moral Quandaries

It's a little trite, but if you can figure out a way to make a superhero choose between saving a helpless innocent—better yet, someone the superhero personally knows and loves—and chasing after you, they'll always go with helping the person in danger. It's one of many reasons having a pit of live, man-eating snails and some rope on hand at basically all times is just a bang-up idea.

Other Distractions

It's certainly smart to have some henchmen on hand to throw at your adversaries, but if you can spare them, also send a few out into the city to bust a water main or take over police HQ at the very instant you're about to take that knockout blow. Or better yet, call up one of your local supervillain colleagues and ask them to put one of their plans in action on the same day as yours.* Give the superheroes something else to do that seems more urgent than your middling cash grab or attempt to turn a major bridge into a portal or madness dimension.

WORST PRACTICE IN ACTION:
The Joker's Ultimate Escape

In their last-ever meeting—or at least, when they both were in their 50s—Batman decided he'd had enough of the Joker and broke his neck. A pretty stunning defeat for the clown prince of crime, right? Well, the Joker just wouldn't have it. So, while laughing his little head off, the Joker twisted his own neck around even further until he was dead, framing Batman for his death.

Teaching Moment: Even when it looks like your arch-nemesis has you dead to rights, there's always a way to one-up the hero. Plus, it's pretty well established that if you die, you're going to come back. So it's a legitimate escape route. If you have to go there, go there.

---

* More on this in Chapter 4.

Timing

In the heat of the moment, it can be a little tough to really know when to stomp the brakes on a plan you've been putting together for months, maybe even years if you just served some time in Laser Jail.* Is it the moment a superhero shows up to stop you? The second they escape your death trap? Should you wait until that hero has cleared your defenses and is on their way to your Control Hub? It's hard to give a hard-and-fast rule here, since so many evil plans are

---

* You never hear about Laser Jail on the news, because the media has agreed to the Superhero-Industrial Complex's requests to keep it secret, but most supervillains end up there nowadays. Think of regular jail, but add lasers. That's pretty much how it is.

different—for instance, some involve sending the superhero to the wrong place so that you'll have more time to send the downtown area underground is a good example.

So I'll say this: If a superhero gets the opportunity to lay you out, odds are they will. Let's face it, they're just plain stronger in most cases; to the point of having an unfair advantage. I mean, really, how is irradiating one's muscles to gargantuan proportions any safer or better than taking illegal steroids? It's a double standard, and they are all assholes.

Anyway, don't let them get to that point. Bounce out of there before it's even much of a possibility; there will be other plans. But you'll have to wait that much longer to enact them if you have to cool it in Laser Jail, or in the cases of some superheroes who have gone to work in the past decade or two, death (which you will come back from—it's a serious revolving door down there, but it's also a huge hassle) for five to ten.

Managing the Fallout

Now that you have made every effort to save your life and your freedom, it's time to turn all your efforts toward ensuring that your reputation as an evildoer remains intact. The last thing you ever want is to be tagged as some sort of . . . not a coward, necessarily. A loser. A failure. An also-ran. Defeated.

But . . . well . . . you have been more or less defeated. So your challenge here is to essentially fight the truth, or at least a version of it. But look, we're supervillains. When the truth is at odds with our purposes—and it very often is—we make it our business to pound the truth into an unrecognizable pulp. In fact, we've perfected the procedure. It takes a little finesse—some smooth moves here and there—but it's definitely achievable.

As famous proto-supervillain George Washington[*] once said, "I cannot tell a lie." He couldn't because he had just hacked the truth (a superhero disguised as a cherry tree) to shit with an ax. Follow his example with these methods:

Play the Victim

The reason I didn't want to use the word "coward" earlier is that this method is perhaps the most cowardly thing anyone can do . . . but it also proves pretty effective. From jail or your headquarters, broadcast yourself speechifying about how you, an honest, hardworking businessperson/entrepreneur/environmentalist/social activist/peace lover, were simply attempting to build a healthier, safer city by encasing it in a giant dome. Some vigilantes out there say you were trying to trap everyone and maybe make them fight until one of them asked for the merciful embrace of death, which you denied (but that was just some wild speculation). It was never your intent! And they, the superheroes, stole the pleasure of dome life from you, the hard-working citizen. True, this method won't cement anyone's reputation as a ruthless evildoer, but it'll certainly get the people on your side. Play it really well, and you might even get them to question their loyalty to the superheroes.

Score a Minor Victory

You may lose the war, but if you can manage to win a battle—maybe you don't manage to put the city under a giant dome,

---

[*] See *The Supervillain Handbook* for more details regarding Washington's days in the early goings of organized super-evil. He was a card, let me tell you.

but you do manage to put city hall in a plastic bubble for a couple of weeks, or flip over a few buildings as you speed away in your rocket escape pod—you can't possibly be a *complete* loser. So always include something in your plans that are totally doable, and wave the flag of victory until you're red in the face.

Talk the Talk

You know how people say that if you repeat something enough times, everyone will believe it? Put it to the test. Repeatedly tell everyone—the public, the press, your enemies, your peers—that you are the most dangerous supervillain who ever lived. It won't matter how many times you lose, it'll still be seared into their brains. (This will be doubly true if you use some hot brands to literally sear it into people's brains. Look into it.)

Cool Off, Sharpen Your Edge, and Make a Comeback

If your recent loss is just too embarrassing, go underground for a few months. Get a new, darker, more intense costume. Bulk up. Maybe replace one or more of your hands with a giant hook or scythe, and return to the scene as an edgier version of yourself. Everyone will automatically forget your previous defeats and stand in awe of your dark, edgy new persona.

Look Better by Comparison

If things get really desperate, arrange for another supervillain (an independent who you don't like very much) to take an even more embarrassing fall to steal the headlines away from you. You can even get one of your henchmen to pose as a superhero and pants them in public.

Say Something Really Smart in Public

This will convince people that you're really smart.

Brainwash Everyone into Believing You Are the Greatest Possible Threat to Their Safety

This is a really useful thing to do, no kidding.

Defeated by Teenagers: Avoiding the Scandal

People new to the super-evil game tend to experience a little bit of shock when they realize just how many of the superheroes they fight on a day-to-day basis are idiot, punk kids. Some are college-age. Some are even younger than that.

It's bad enough to get your clock cleaned by an adult flying around the world with a pompadour on their head and some bright-red tights on. Imagine what it feels like to get laid out by a high school sophomore. Yet many supervillains have dealt with that exact type of trauma, and not only lived through it, but have weathered it without any permanent damage to their status as evildoers. I asked one such supervillain, a fellow by the name of The Comptroller, to describe his experience:

Your enemy.

I used to pull these jobs where I'd confuse the dickens out of people in various levels of government and business by talking to them about revenue percentage gains in the fiscal year, and then I'd clean out their safes while they were—to put it in layman's terms— mumbo-jumboed unconscious.

It was all really great work until this group of kids, I think they called themselves The Minor Chords, caught onto what I was doing and started waking up my victims by playing this really dour rock music. They were impervious to my attacks, since financials meant absolutely nothing to them, and therefore they couldn't be incapacitated with it. And their leader, Ema—that was her name, just Ema—would pick me up and drop me down a smokestack. She would do this every single time. I think she thought it was funny, but she never laughed. I never saw her laugh. They were all pretty weird kids.

Anyway, I started getting really worried that all my business associates and, you know, other independent contractors who do our sort of work, would start to view me in an unfavorable light. I was nearly forty years old, being thrown down smokestacks nearly every other week by this kid who couldn't have been a day over seventeen. It worried me for a while.

After a few months, though, I developed a system; one where I could continue to occasionally lose to the young superheroes and still come out looking like I didn't deserve to be on the Z-list. I worked it out pretty easy. Here's the secret: Don't talk about them like they're teenagers. Tell everyone they're adults. That may sound unbelievable, but it isn't. It really isn't!

See, these kids, when they get superpowers, they bulk up. They get big, they look like they're grown-ups. And unless they're sidekicking, they even give themselves adult names. You know, names that end in '–Man,' or start with 'Captain.' They don't want anybody to know they're really adolescents. The only way anybody would know is if you told them! I very nearly made this mistake.

So if, for some crazy reason, your teenage adversary is trying to smash up your lair using a name that makes it clear he or she is a teen—mine sure didn't—tell 'em it's embarrassing for them that they're using that name. People'll think they're kids! They'll give in to peer pressure and change it in a second.

So that's it. If a teenager keeps beating you up every week, tell everyone they're about twenty-eight. That'll fix everything right up.

Okay. I told you everything. Can I leave now? Can I . . . hey, can I leave now, King? I cooperated! I told my secret! I retired from this supervillain stuff! You can't leave me down here! Come on! Why are you doing th—"

So there you have it! A simple way to keep teenagers from making you a laughing stock, unless you're dumb enough to tell everyone who was anyone in supervillainy about it in a book they're all going to read.

You deserve to be in there, Comptroller, you teenage-beating-taking idiot.

Chapter 3

When You Win

Like I said before, the deck in this game is stacked against you. Tons of people are rooting for you to lose, and they'll rig the game as thoroughly as they can to see a superhero seize victory.* But every once in a while, when a plan is laid out exactly right, with every "T" crossed and every "I" dotted, when the stars align in perfect order and maybe the superheroes get into an argument with each other about who's the saddest, you finally pull out a win.

It's a hell of a moment. Think about an Olympic gold medalist standing on the podium, their hand over their heart, their country's flag reaching toward the ceiling as the national anthem plays for everyone in the stadium. Tears well up in their eyes as the culmination of a lifetime of work and dedication comes together in the most glorious moment of their lives. Now imagine someone shrinking that stadium down to the size of a peanut and feeding it to an elephant, just to see the Olympic stadium get pooped out later. Wouldn't that be awesome to pull off? That's what a supervillain victory feels like.

A lot of people never get to experience that feeling because they aren't me (if you haven't figured it out yet, I never lose). But, occasionally, things happen for them.

---

* And yet, it's the superheroes that always brood and whine and act like they aren't having any fun. They are just disgusting.

Supervillain FAQ: What's the evilest way to travel?

We can't all benefit from the powers of portal generation, the ability to travel through mirrors, reality manipulation, or even super-speed and flight. Some of us have to motor.

But how to best get around? This depends on your style, and on which setbacks you're most willing to endure.

Consider these options:

A Car

Are you a street-level type of person? Do you hate fancy things that travel in the air or on water? Are you on a very limited budget? A quick paint job, some body modifications, and the addition of wheel spikes to an old Toyota Tercel should cover you.

A Motorcycle

Do you wish you got more bugs in your mouth while driving a car? Here's your answer. Also: Popping wheelies is awesome.

Your Own Train

Beautifully ostentatious and severely impractical. Pretty damn perfect for a supervillain. Just be sure, though, that you don't really want to go anywhere but lumberyards and warehouses.

A Tank

Steady, strong, and heavily armed. Not a bad choice, but not well-suited for getaways. Also, superheroes love bending tank guns to show off how strong they are. It's really like their favorite thing to do. So beware of that.

A Private Plane or Helicopter

Great for villains who like to escape by jumping onto hanging rope ladders or driving a motorcycle into a docking bay. Also appeals to those villains who outright don't give one single damn about air traffic rules (which is most of us).

A Hovering Glider

If your supervillain name has the word "goblin" in it, you're contractually required to use one of these. So get on it.

A Jetpack

Mind having feet that are on fire? Because your feet will almost always be on fire. Though you'll be the envy of anyone who complains about it not yet being the future.

A Boat

There are lots of places to rob on the coast, rivers, fjords, by inlets, in and around lakes, or in sounds. If you have no interest in committing crimes in places other than those, go for this.

A Submarine

All the limitations of a boat, plus inner-ear pain.
But hey, torpedoes!

Teleportation Devices

You may not have the power to teleport yourself,
but that doesn't mean you can't kidnap some brai-
niac to fix up a machine for you. But make sure
this braniac is someone who knows how to make
teleportation devices.*

A Balloon of Some Sort

Balloons look awesome. They're huge, they look
super-imposing, and you can adorn them with
spikes and all kinds of other intimidating shit to
really up the ante. Plus, you're just up there, hov-
ering over everyone, making them wonder what

---

*   There's currently no one who can do this. At least, no one I'm willing to
    tell you about.

you're going to drop on them. (My suggestion would be some kind of especially pungent stink bomb. That's nothing but fun.) The downside? It's a balloon. It can be popped. Somebody's probably going to pop it. Weighed against all the cool parts, it's a tough call.

A Rocket Ship
Excellent, if precise landings are not in your top ten travel requirements. Also, rather lengthy takeoffs.

A Plain Old Rocket
Do you wish you got more birds in your mouth when you're flying a rocket ship? Here's your answer. Jump right on top of this sucker and go.

A Rocket-Powered Skateboard
On the one hand, it'd be very fun to ride around. On the other, Rocket Racer can be a real litigious cat about his calling card. Watch out for him.

A Giant, Tank-Like, Mechanical Spider
I can honestly think of no potential problems with this vehicle. It's basically perfect.

Of course, it would be far too easy for the battle to be over when you finally shame that superhero that's been a thorn in your side for years, sending them into exile or into the ground and taking over your immediate area. Not only do you have to actually make some decisions while you're in charge,* you also have to handle yourself in a winnerly way. Going too far off the deep end with a celebration is almost certainly going to result in some sort of ironic-yet-deserved comeuppance coming at you tout suite.

Avoid tempting the hand of Fate, that cheap bastard. Cheer, but cheer prudently. As my old mentor, Dr. Blattarius, used to say, "Waving your arms around like some kind of happy person is an easy way to get kicked in the junk."

---

* See Chapter 9

What to Do

Gloating

The first thing you're going to want to do when you finally smash The Masked Mightyman or one of his "friends" with a giant mallet is to start shouting at the heavens about how you knew this day would come, and that you are the greatest and most brilliant force of badness that has ever lived. You may think I'm going to tell you that you shouldn't do that,* but I quite enthusiastically encourage this.

Here's why. Words are cheap. It doesn't cost you much of anything to say them, and while you're in celebration mode, there are likely going to be some people who aren't otherwise inclined to listen to you who may perk up their ears. Wiping out a superhero team by infiltrating them with a secret robot member you control, or successfully sending your city back to the sixteenth century is a damn effective way of getting some attention.

Seize That Attention

Look, if nothing else, you'll build up your rep for being a supervillain to contend with. Like I said in Chapter 2, the more times you repeat something, the more inclined people will be to believe it. That's especially true if your most recent act is one that, no shit, succeeded. Milk it. Go on every news channel. Hold huge public events at stadiums. Appoint your henchmen to radio stations you forcefully take over, so they can talk about you on air. Fly dirigibles over the city with your name written on them. Put up loudspeakers everywhere that repeat over and over, at all hours of the day, that you are the supreme power. You'll be creating more insomniacs, who

---

* I know you think that, because I own your thoughts. You remember.

are constantly thinking about you and your various rays of fluctuating temperatures all night long.

Eliminating other Threats

Experiencing victory often gives supervillains (and anyone else who is egotistically inclined) the feeling that they're invincible and cannot be touched by anyone. You should know that it's actually quite the contrary. A major consequence of winning is that you, with the one harmless act of severely maiming a superhero or turning the city's government buildings and officials into Legos®, are putting a giant target on your back. Huge. Everyone's going to want to come after you. Superheroes from all over the world, other supervillains, what's left of the police, the National Guard, the UN, the Space Cops,* you name it.

So what do you do? My suggestion would be to round up as many of those people as you can and put them in a gulag of some sort, preferably as far away from you as they can possibly be. Maybe one that's also microscopically small? Just throwing out ideas here.

Your other option is to bunker down in a nigh-impenetrable fortress, surrounded by loyal lackeys who are willing to take the harshest of sound-barrier breaking punches and the shiniest of Space Cop asteroid glitter attacks for you.

Prepare for Your Loyal Lackeys to Turn on You

Maybe they'll envy your position of power. Maybe they'll grow tired of the constant gloating that you should be doing

---

* Oh yeah, there are Space Cops. They're basically like other cops, but there from space and enforce space laws. They have weird faces and sometimes have tentacles for arms. They're generally idiots.

all the time and not even thinking about. Maybe they're simply taking advantage of the first time that you've slept outside of a vacuum-sealed chamber in nearly a decade (more on that in a bit). Whatever the reason, you're bound to have a few good apples in the bunch who want to spoil everything. Alert your henchmen and the other denizens of your lair and/or fortress to be on the lookout for any funny business.

You should make sure to tell them, "If you see something, say something . . . or you'll never see or say ever again . . . or hear or feel or taste." They should take the hint that they'll be dead for disobeying you. That should be clear enough.

Eat Some Cake

See? I'm not entirely inhuman and focused on business. Indulge in some cake, you've earned it. (Check it for poison, though. And probably stand up while you're eating. Also, *damnation*, make sure it's chocolate. Vanilla is a bullshit hero flavor and you know it. Have some standards, for Christ's sake.)

CONGRATULATIONS! YOU DESTROYED OUR LIVES

WORST PRACTICE IN ACTION:
Kraven Buries His Enemy

There was this one time that Kraven the Hunter shot Spider-Man and buried him. Like, beat him cold. It was amazing. Kraven's response was a little odd; he dressed up as Spider-Man and went around the city trying to prove he was better in every conceivable way. But, hey, it's a form of gloating. Of course Spider-Man eventually was revived (Kraven shot him with a tranquilizer because he wanted to prove to Spider-Man's face he was his better), and Kraven called it quits as his enemy's better.

Teaching Moment: Kraven figured out a way to go out like a boss: as a winner. If you can manage this (preferably without messily killing yourself like Kraven had to), then go for it.

What Not to Do
Relax

In addition to feeling invincible, winners also tend to get these wild notions in their heads that, with one mark in the "W" column, they've somehow gained license to sleep like a normal human being or sit down in a chair that isn't covered with live grenades. Those people are kidding themselves! I should have made it abundantly clear to you by now that everyone who could have any interest in coming after you will do so once they get word of your triumph.

The only thing winning should do is make you even more inclined to sleep with one eye open, and preferably, mounted on the outside of your headquarters where you can see the surrounding area from a decent vantage point. (We've got a guy who can do detachable eyes. Let me know if you're interested.) Any relaxation you do should be in a sealed chamber that only you can enter and leave. And it won't hurt to create a clone of yourself to watch over you while you sleep, as long as you can ensure that you can easily self-destruct that sucker the second they start making dollar-sign eyes at you. (Like I said, clones are just terrible.)

Overreach

You may be inclined to think that you can pull off an even bigger plan once you've succeeded with one. Like, maybe this time you can threaten another, larger city with an even bigger sentient case of gonorrhea, and take it over. Hold that thought, Cheetah-O.*

Now is no time to go on offense; at least, not physically. You can attack with words all you want, but shifting your attention to anything but spatial defense right now is sure folly. Superheroes in other cities are going to amass against you and take you down the moment you're most vulnerable. You'll look like an imbecile and lose all the bad will you've gained from your victory. Plus, when you're acting, you're not talking, and you remember how I am about that. Don't test me.

---

* If you haven't heard of him, Cheetah-O is a man whose DNA got crossed with a cheetah and a Cheeto. He's got the speed of a cheetah and the orange, cheese-flavored dust of a Cheeto. When he runs away, he blinds everyone with cheese dust. He's fast. That's why I made the reference.

Expect the Superhero You Vanquished to Stay That Way

You think we're the only ones who don't stay dead or otherwise incapacitated? Superheroes come back all the time, my delusional friend. They are real bastards that way. So get in your rep-building where you can, eat that piece of cake standing up, and keep an eye on the news. The second you hear that your arch-nemesis has miraculously returned from whatever fate you resigned them to, blow out of there for a while. Head underground, underwater, or to another dimension for a month or two. Let that musclebrain cool off for a spell, because they always come back mad. Dying or being sent to a psychological wasteland of unspeakable terrors really sends them overboard for some weird reason.

Then, when you're hiding out, that's when you can have a nice nap.

Blast That Bias: How to Spin Beating the "Good Guys"

People are weird. They tend to get all protective of superheroes just because they save an elderly relative of theirs from getting crushed by the door of a bank vault, or they put some giant sculpture back on top of a building after you knock it off with a helicopter, or they manage to stop the river of lava coming down Main Street, or they stop the Main Street you brought to life from extinguishing a friendly lava monster. It's a really strange inclination people have.

So when you send one of those precious heroes to their doom, some folks really go off the deep end. They get all up on the TV to talk about how you've ruined society as we know it or they'll write articles about how you should be removed from your throne atop the Hellspire you summoned to the center of the city. Sometimes, they have problems with Hellspires, too. No accounting for taste, I guess.

In some ways, those wrongheaded people are doing your job for you. They're spreading the word about your infamous and destructive deeds, almost certainly informing people who only had a vague idea of your evil about the depths of dastardliness you can truly achieve. But here's the deal: You sort of have to manage this stuff. Keeping people paralyzed with fear is great. The thing you have to avoid is mobilizing them. Nobody's going to benefit from a huge mob of regular schmucks charging at your lair in the middle of the night. That's merely another hassle to deal with.

How do you strike that balance? The key is to keep people afraid, but try to keep them from becoming enraged, with stuff like this:

Dig Up Some Dirt on the Superhero You Defeated and Make It Public

Maybe she cheated on her husband one time or he constantly scolded people for not eating the low-fat version of some snack food. Whatever it is, make sure the superhero looks like a hypocrite, nitpicker, or just an unpleasant person to hang out with. It doesn't even have to be anything major. People are vindictive as hell. They'll lose their boners for any big-name role model in a second, based on any minor, perceived slight against them. They're more like us than they think, really.

Make Up Some Dirt

If, in the event that you can find absolutely nothing incriminating about the superhero in question (and, really, there's bound to be *something*; really dig and then dig harder), make something up. Sure, it'll get refuted later, but for now, during your moment of victory, you'll be able to slide it past them. They ate some puppies, maybe? See how far you can go.*

Stage a Stunt

Send a bus full of "children" (your henchmen) careening off a cliff. Rig up some special effects so that you can convincingly swoop in and save them, even if you can't fly or don't have super strength. (It honestly doesn't matter whether the henchmen get hurt or not. Really, who cares?) Make sure every reporter in the city is there to see it. Oh ho ho, who's the hero now?**

---

* More on maligning the character of superheroes and other do-gooders in Chapter 6.

** Of course, the risk you're taking here is that people may actually start to like you rather than fear you. That's a dilemma I'll dig into a little deeper in Chapter 9.

Make Careful Use of a Plant
You know how I said you should have your henchmen host all the local radio shows talking about how scary you are? You can take that one step further. Post some of your henchmen at radio stations and TV stations, posing as hosts and anchors, and have them say, in no uncertain terms, that it's an awful idea to come after you right now. You'll probably blow everyone up! It's not cool being blown up, either, so they should probably just stay home all the time, for perpetuity.

Silence the Shit-Stirrers
You know the ones. Those few voices that really get people riled up, inspire them to push past their fears, and take action. Literally shoot a silencing ray right into their mouths. That should take care of it. You'll know which ones are doing the riling because of all their screaming and stuff. Shouldn't be too hard.

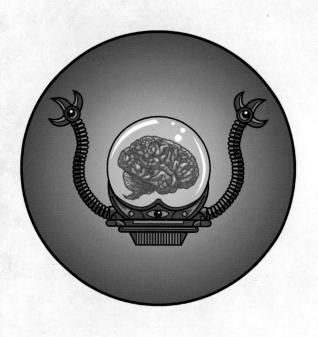

Chapter 4

Making Alliances

Most times, supervillainy is a solitary profession. It's true that you have to surround yourself with dozens—if not hundreds—of slack-jawed idiots you call henchmen basically every day, but you can't really call them peers or turn to them as confidants or even really think of them as people. They are *resources*. Like, I don't know, timber. Timber may be a little smarter, though.

Anyway, my point is that you don't generally work with others on a regular basis; unlike superheroes, who will team up at literally the slightest provocation. They can run into each other at the grocery store and decide to team up to buy eggs. It's sickening. Superheroes also have sidekicks, which, while quite obviously worryingly dangerous for the teenagers, and sometimes children, involved,* does at least offer some form of companionship.† Then, of course, there are the superhero teams; those groups of weirdly-powered stray puzzle pieces who don't necessarily have what it takes to fight crime themselves, but can join forces with a few others to make it work. Or there are those super-teams of nothing but heavy hitters that are patently ridiculous and unfair. Those who are invincible or are, like,

---

* Can you really trust a guy in a rubber mask who voluntarily goes out at night to sit on a rooftop, looking for people to punch, to look out for their safety?

† Plus, it gives us an easy target to kidnap so we can really get under the superhero's skin. And honestly, whose fault is it that a child was standing around in an alley where anybody could freeze her and take her to an Antarctic base?

mythical gods, don't really need to hang out with seven other similarly overpowered brutes just to smash robots. That's flat-out absurd.

Supervillains tend to work outside of such pairings or groups, unlike the superheroes who always say they "work alone," but really have like thirty different people who work with them all the time. However, sometimes, one of those ridiculous, heroic super-teams shows up at your doorstep. Occasionally, a plan calls for more than one set of hands/ skills/brains/playfully themed bombs. Every now and again you need a time machine but don't have one, and you know FutureFop, the ruffed dandy from the forty-fifth century, has one.* That's when you have to hold your nose and work with . . . ugh . . . other supervillains.

I can't stand the young'uns, but there's one way supervillains are a lot like modern-day hipsters: No, not in that we all wear tight pants that barely come halfway up our calves and weird kerchiefs and pretend we can understand what Bon Iver is saying (though his music does make a great hypnotism primer; play only a few minutes and most people will be so cross-eyed and confused that they'll be open to basically any suggestion). The similarity is that we, although sharing very specific traits that clearly identify us as a group, often *hate* one another.

Call it petty—because it is—but it's weird to see other people doing what you do in an ever-so-slightly different way. Most often in a way that leaves out some idiosyncratic tic that you find necessary to do your work. Maybe they dress just a little bit differently. Maybe they favor giant,

---

* In case you were curious, this is the only reason anyone has ever opted to work with FutureFop.

irradiated snakes over giant, irradiated lizards.* Maybe they laugh weird; or maybe they were one of your former employees who you "fired" by blowing up the building they worked in and leaving them to die. There are lots of little, nitpicky reasons.

Supervillain FAQ: Should I go into politics?

Those of you who aren't monarchs of tiny European countries that people always think are fictional for some reason** often raise the question of whether it's worthwhile to reach out for a so-called legitimate power, either in business or in the world of absurd theater known as politics.

For some perspective on whether entering the arena of government can be of any use to those seeking the systematic destruction of everything the average citizen holds dear, I turned to Senatrix Restraint, a five-term state senator and life long pain dealer, to see whether she'd do it all over again if she could.

You know, it's an interesting question. A while back in the fifties and sixties, it was a lot easier to freak people out. People like the Congressmangler and others in that first handful of masks that managed to win elections really

_____

** You son of a bitch, Explosia is real, and I have a crown to prove it!

_____

* They're both wrong, by the way. It's giant, irradiated apes or nothing.

broke some barriers for us. When he made his first speech on the floor of the House, the one where he told all the other reps that he was going to use a reality transmogrification machine to reshape all their districts so that they'd become his district that all their constituents would become his constituents, and with that he'd be able to make them perform in wrestling matches as he commanded, I mean, that was history in the making right there.

It's harder to get noticed now. Every time you turn around these days, somebody's threatening to cut off food supplies this or wants to seal the air off to maternity wards that. It's next to impossible to stand out. A couple of weeks ago, I gave this speech on the Senate floor about how I wanted to make this one county a crater because a store clerk there was rude to me. Hardly anyone panicked at all. Just fifteen or even ten years ago, you would have gotten, at the very least, some screaming from the gallery.

So I don't know how much of a career boost it is anymore. I will say, though, that it's not the hill to climb it used to be, either. Fifty years ago, it was a challenge and a chore to win votes as an 'out' supervillain, mask and all. Lots of the early bad-guy candidates had to run under the guise of being hero-friendly, revealing themselves as villains on Inauguration Day by holding everyone in attendance hostage and revealing the judge who swore them in to be a Frankenstein.

Here in the second decade of the twenty-first century, supervillains are often the lesser of two evils when they're running against plain old politicians. Seizing power has never been easier. It's that you can't really get the attention you used to. That's the thing.

Plus, it's tough to get your colleagues, even other supervillains, to vote for any of your bills. You know how that goes. You want to drain a lake and fill it with blood, and they'd prefer to turn the water into sulfuric acid. So you end up compromising and making it a lake of urine; an outcome no one wanted.

That's just politics, I guess.

Oh, hey, by the way, what's that creepy weirdo The Comptroller doing in here? And why is his mouth wired shut? Is he in some kind of trouble with the Society? I mean, I always thought the guy was kind of strange, but—hey! Why is this big metal door closing? What's going on! I have committee meetings to get to!

Heeeeyyyyy!

Politicians, am I right? Always stretching the truth about being imprisoned after interviews on whether their political careers have helped them in the world of evil. Anyway, take what she said as you may, potential makers of evil laws.

Whatever the reason, these little details irk us. Supervillains are detail-oriented people by nature, and we also have tons of weird quirks that tend to come out because of what "professionals" call "insanity." It's often those quirks that make us who we are, upon which we base our entire identity; so being around someone who you think might belittle that or impose some quirk of their own on how you do things? That's trouble.

That's why it's imperative that you ensure a few things as you move forward with any supervillain alliance. For one thing, *never be part of a group you didn't start.** You will get crushed.

And if you do opt to start one, do all this stuff first:

Know You're Smarter than Your Recruits

Yes, you should constantly be riding high on hubris and egotism because that's the supervillain way, but in cases like this, really do your research.

What sorts of plans have they tried to pull off?

If they've done some published writing, how good is it? (The book you're holding is an example of the "universally lauded as brilliant" category, for reference.)

When they talk, do they say things that go over your head?

If you answered "yes" to any of these questions, this person will definitely outwit and screw you over somehow . . . and I don't mean in like an egotistical or hubristic sort of way.

Even so, it's also important that you don't hire total fools, either. They need to be open to any of your suggestions (i.e., commands), but also quick enough on their feet to get themselves out of a scrape if you're not around.

---

* Unless I'm starting it, then you'll be totally fine. I promise.

So have a vetting process. Hire some attorneys to do the digging for you. (Also, vet the attorneys to make sure they won't outsmart you somehow. Get some attorneys to look into their backgrounds.)

Have Contingency Plans

Remember how I said that supervillains almost always hate one another? That's often because we don't very much like the idea of splitting our winnings with anyone else. Or our glory. Or our lunch. We don't really like sharing in general. So you should prepare yourself, before you even ask anyone to help you for a mutiny. Figure out effective ways to subdue your allies if they become too hard to handle, because they will knock you down and take your football (or football-shaped Universe Eraser Device) in a second if they get the chance.

Some ways in which you might consider doing this:

- Implant them with a chip that you say will boost their strength, but actually electrifies their brain stems when you push a button;
- Keep a vial filled with a liquefied version of their one weakness on hand at all times;
- Throw them at the superhero at the first sign of a red cape;
- Put their chair at the conference table over a trap-door portal to hell;
- Have henchmen constantly stand behind them to tie their shoelaces together at a moment's notice;
- Or be ready to just plain disintegrate them if they mess with you.

WORST PRACTICE IN ACTION:
The Injustice League

Led by space conqueror Agamemno, this team, which included Lex Luthor, Sinestro, Catwoman, Dr. Light, Black Manta, Penguin, and others, nearly defeated the Justice League by switching bodies with them. It was only when the Green Lantern figured out a way to reverse the mind-swap that things sort of fell apart. Even then, they had an advantage against the heroes by having spent time in their bodies.**

Teaching Moment: You can't switch bodies with every member of a superhero team yourself, even if it would be much more palatable if you could.

** They also knew exactly what all their genitals looked like.

Assert Your Authority

Before anybody says a word, you need to act in such a way that makes it very clear you're the one in charge. You may think that you've already asserted that simply by being the one who gathered the group together, but you could not be more mistaken. Everyone, even the dumbest supervillain you bring to the table, is going to jockey for a leadership position and assume they are the best suited for the job.

So how can you make sure the team knows you're the one wearing the pants (even if you're wearing some sort of toga or tunic or ribbed, metal leggings)? Stand up and slice the conference table* in half, preferably with a chop of your own forearm. If you don't have any martial arts skill to speak of, a sword or an energy blade will suffice. Then take the remains of that table and throw them out the window.† Then, say this:

> The very idea of the members of this gathering sitting at a table offends me. That table may indeed have had a head at which a leader could sit, but we all would still have been on the same level. You all will sit. I will float above you. You will do what I tell you.

Then have some henchmen come in and hold you above their heads for the rest of the meeting. . . . Unless you really can float; that would be even more imposing. However you raise yourself up, this should do a reasonably effective job— at least at first—of making it pretty clear that you're not just the chairperson, but the float person of this committee of chaos.

Make It an Odd Number

I know they're famous and all, but the Sinister Six really should have been the Sinful Seven or the Foul Five. Why? For the same reason that both the Supreme Court and the

---

*   I should have mentioned that it's important to have everyone meet in some sort of conference room. Not because you're trying to make it businessy, but more so you can pull off this authority-asserting maneuver.
†   Oh yeah, right. Make sure it's a conference room with some big windows.

Wu-Tang Clan have nine members: Every vote needs a tie-breaker. Of course, in a conglomeration of supervillains, everyone is a leg-breaker, which is also one of our preferred ways of settling ties. To avoid the inevitable deadlocks that will occur in the few and far between times you'll actually allow your colleagues to take a vote, it's downright necessary to have that tiebreaking vote at the (non) table. (Wait to break everyone else's legs until the job is *over*.) It's also imperative that that vote always side with you. Which is why you must . . .

Have a Patsy

What if everything falls apart? Certainly you don't want to go in anticipating failure, but come on; look at the morons you have to work with. And yet, it's likely that you're the person everyone is going to blame when things go wrong; only because you asserted complete ideological and tactical control over the entire operation. People are always trying to pin it on a scapegoat.

That's why you need one person in the group who is constantly under your thumb during the entire caper—the one who always breaks ties in your favor, the one who repeats a lot of what you say, the one who laughs really hard at all your jokes—the one whom everyone else would call your lapdog. Maybe this person is another respectable supervillain you brainwashed and brought in to convince everyone your plan was legitimately going to be profitable for them; maybe it's a henchman you've temporarily promoted to supervillain status for this one week only to bust them back down to toilet brush duty (that's not toilet cleaning duty; this is when you force them to put on bristled hats and be the brush themselves) immediately after; maybe it's a hologram of someone who's stashed away in a closet somewhere.

Whoever this person is, it needs to be someone that, if it comes down to it, you can plausibly blame everything on.

- Oh, it seemed like they were always voting in your favor? It was actually their idea every time!
- They jumped up and planted a bug in your ear, and you suggested it. They're repeating what you say?
  That's because they're making sure you're getting out their plans word-for-word, like someone mouthing song lyrics!
- They laughed at all your jokes?
  Well, you are pretty witty.

Pin everything back on the patsy and leave the group in shambles, without any of the blame touching you.

In case you were curious about what other types of villains you need to have in your alliance (you know, besides the patsy), it obviously depends on the plan—heists and demolition missions obviously would need completely different skill sets—but in a general sense, here are some all-around types it's smart to have around:

A Leader

This is you. Be smart.

A Punching Bag

Someone who can absorb gobs of superhero fists so

Make everyone immediately aware that you're the boss.

you and the other players in the game can avoid unwanted tooth, bone, or vital organ loss. Healing powers, invulnerability, and/or the ability to make multiple versions of oneself are valuable.

An Infiltrator

Someone who can slide into a place that is heavily guarded and zip right out, unnoticed. This allows for large portions of heists to be accomplished while the rest of the team gets thoroughly hammered. Invisibility and stretching powers are valuable.

A Heavy Hitter

Sometimes you have to make stuff blow up, so find someone who naturally makes stuff blow up. Pyrokinetic and combustive powers are valuable.

An Escape Enabler

There are teams that can teleport away from situations and there are those that can't. Don't be the latter. So what's valuable here is, quite obviously, teleportation. Maybe flight.

A Gadget Hoarder

You never know when you might need a device that makes mummies come to life or makes people want to eat their own teeth. You never know.

A Weirdo

While this team member is distracting any nearby superheroes by reciting passages from *Faust* while smothering his or herself in chicken blood, you can otherwise go about your business. All this person needs is to be insane.

A Job Badly Done: Taking All the Credit

I've covered how you should wrest control of any group projects away from the other supervillains you've recruited onto your team and how to pass the blame to some idiot if things don't work out . . . but if things do work out, though? You want to be the one who takes home the trophy. I mean the figurative trophy. It'll probably be something like the United Kingdom shrunk down and stuffed into a bottle or a vial of powder that used to be your enemy or, you know, a whole lot of money. But you get the idea.

You also want everyone to know that it was you—not any of those other people that were involved—who masterminded everything.

And also made all the major tactical decisions.

And won all the fights!

And saved all those other idiots' asses when they almost ruined everything!

Basically, what you want is to make it seem like you brought in these other members along just to have an audience for your amazing supervillainous exploits. Of course, the other members of the team are going to want to get some sort of "credit" for their "contributions," and that's if you're lucky. Odds are they're all going to want to steal the glory that's so clearly yours.

You have some options for how to act to take your deserved victory lap. Some may work better than others, so choose carefully between these courses of action:

As soon as the Job Is Complete, Shoot Everyone Else on the Team with a Silencing Ray So They Cannot Speak

This way, you can tell the *real* story without interruption. The only thing about silencing rays is that they're almost never permanent.

Slander Their Names

It's not going to take all that much work to get people to believe a cabal of criminals is full of lazy, good-for-nothing liars and credit hogs. (Sometimes, we can use our untrustworthy reputations to our advantage.) So get out there and make people believe it. But what if there was one supervillain who was also a hard worker and who told people the truth about how they single-handedly did everything? Have the courage to be this person.

Creative Editing

Record and/or photograph everything you do, then just edit or use Photoshop to make yourself the clear driver of all activity. The only downside here is that you're actually recording evidence of your own highly illegal activities, but it's probably worth it.

Distract

As you're putting a bow on your big, team plan, arrange it so all your compatriots have to deal with some big problem—maybe they get stuck in a sealed room for two weeks or they are attacked by fifteen new "superheroes" who are really your henchmen—that you conveniently avoid having to deal with somehow. Now you've got plenty of time to get the real truth out there.

Kill 'Em

You probably won't need them again. And you're all supervillains. They had to know this was probably coming.**

** More on this in the next chapter.

Chapter 5

Dissolving Alliances

Unless you experienced a memory wipe in the time since you've read the previous chapter—and look, I know that shit happens; you point the brain scrambler the wrong way and accidentally fire, I'm not judging*—you'll recall that I said we supervillains often do not get along. I just looked over your thoughts, which I remind you that I own, and those of you who still have memories are curious about how I have managed to keep the International Society of Supervillains together for so long.

Well, I'll let you in on a little secret.† I am the only perpetual member of the ISS. I'm like Lemmy from Motörhead.‡ I am the band . . . and the brand.

If other members of your group aren't recognizing your authority or trying to write their own songs or get a cut of the money, kick them out. Get a new drummer and bass player and replace them with guys that have brains inside of glass skulls. Who cares who's filling those positions? As

---

* This is a lie. *Of course* I'm judging. I'm always judging.
† But I'll have to kill you as soon as you read it. Mwa ha ha! I'm only jokin', I'll only have to kill some of you.
‡ In case you didn't know, Lemmy is a supervillain (his supervillain name is quite literally, The Motör Head) and a friend of mine. He is also really amazing to party with.

long as the front man sings "Ace of Spades" the way he's been singing it for thirty years, they'll keep buying. (My equivalent of "Ace of Spades" is turning continents upside-down.)

Like me and Lemmy, you have to know when to kick the other members of the band out and find some new faceless nobodies to take their place. Or, if you're like, I don't know, Phil Collins,* you can branch out and go solo after shedding the husk that is your Genesis.

Supervillain FAQ: Can bad guys fall in love?

While we're sort of on the topic of love. . . . Around holidays like Valentine's Day, when balloons and packages of candy and Sarin gas pellets all come in heart shapes, it's difficult, even for the blackest hearted among us, not to think of loves lost, never found, or accidentally disintegrated.

Many among our ranks often wonder whether it's possible, outside a few notable exceptions— The Joker and Harley Quinn, The Monarch and Dr. Girlfriend, The Absorbing Man and Titania, Bebop and Rocksteady, The Ventriloquist and Scarface—many villains are unlucky when it comes to finding that lifelong alliance we call love.

---

* Also a supervillain (code name: Sussudior), he's less amazing to party with, but his confusion and drumming powers are pretty useful.

But is that the way it has to be? Not necessarily. Follow these basic guidelines, and you may beat the odds:

Present Yourself Well

Walking straight out of your state-of-the-art laboratory for mad science experiments smelling like an attack gator and covered in hypno-gel is no way to attract a mate (unless you plan is to frighten them with attack gators, then subdue your potential mate with hypno-gel). Take a shower. Comb your hair. Put on some nice clothes. Change your appearance using a portable hologram projector. De-age yourself with a Youth Beam. This is simple, basic hygiene.

Find Someone with Common Interests

Lots of cities have supervillain hangouts. Go to one sometime. Chat up a looker with some banter about how this guy you know with the powers of a spider was mean to you at your job once and now you spend every minute of the day trying to kill him. You'll find someone who's interested.

Be Confident

You're a person who spends most of the week making lengthy speeches about how everyone will pay for not respecting you enough. You can ask another human being to go eat food with you sometime.

Be Willing to Open Yourself Up, Emotionally

To develop a lasting relationship, you need to get past your prickly exterior and show the true, sensitive supervillain underneath. The one who acts out just because they want to feel wanted.*

Try to Become Capable of Love

If your first instinct when you're around someone is to give them everything they could want in life, that's pretty close to love. If your first instinct is to swarm them with MurderBots, it isn't.**

Do NOT Kill Your Mate

That's pretty counterproductive, at least in this particular case.

---

* Important Note: PorcuPete, this one is impossible for you.
** But it's a lot like marriage, am I right, folks?

But when do you know it's time for them to head out the door, likely into a phalanx of robots ready to slice them up with laser nets? There are numerous circumstances in which it's just prudent to tell them not to let the door hit them in the ass (then tear the door off the hinges and beat them severely with it). Here's a smattering of scenarios in which you should get to firin':

- Anyone, at any time, suggests someone other than you is in charge of the operation.

- Members of the group suddenly demanding their "fair share," or "a cut," or "meals."
- Disagreements over what to call your association. For example, you want "brotherhood of mayhem," while they want "fraternity of devastation," and those are very important distinctions.
- They insist on matching uniforms, thereby cramping your style and everyone else's.
- They insist on wearing their own special outfit when you have created specific uniforms for everyone.
- They don't show up on time for meetings.
- They show up for meetings too early.
- They show up for meetings on time, but are all whiny about them.
- They ask too many questions.
- They don't ask any questions, thereby showing a lack of interest in the project.
- One of them scrapes your foot with theirs and scuffs your kicks.
- Annoying tongue clicking.
- Annoying pen clicking.
- Perceptions that the other members of the group like someone more than they like you, warranted or not.
- Unsanctioned swagger.
- Sanctioned swagger that goes too far.
- Suspiciously heroic behavior.
- Won't shut up about last night's *Top Chef* episode, when you clearly stated that you haven't seen it yet.

Every last one of these reasons is 100 percent valid justifications for bringing an end to a partnership. But once you have decided to dissolve the agreement, what are the most forceful and authoritative ways to make it happen? It can be a bit of a sticky situation, especially if you have contracts or blood oaths or pacts with demon broods binding you together.*

Even with those binding agreements tying you together, you do have a handful of valid options when you're looking to sever them. Try one of these:

Kill 'Em All

Sometimes, the titles of Metallica albums are places to find the best advice.† As I said in the previous chapter, you'll find that occasionally, the cleanest way to get rid of your problems is also the messiest. Odds are you aren't ever going to need these people again, and even if you need their types, B-list villains with energy powers are literally everywhere nowadays because they've all read my previous book and think they have a chance to actually get somewhere in this business. Also note that supervillains notoriously don't shut up about perceived wrongs other people have done to them. Best to just shut them up permanently (or at least until they're all revived in some big event in which some idiot superhero accidentally raises their corpses from the grave by hitting a wrong button in some old temple).

---

* It's always risky business to work with demon broods. You'd do yourself a favor by opting to avoid them in any situation that doesn't involve fighting a war with some angels; a situation you may be surprised to find yourself in every few years. It happens.

† For example, *Load* and *Reload* are the perfect shorthand way to remember how to use a handgun on an oncoming wave of superheroes. . . . *And Justice For All* doesn't tell you much, though. Screw justice.

Always come armed.

Kill Yourself (Or Fake It)

Say you're committing several murders of people with beyond-human intellects and powers that seem like something beyond your capabilities. Maybe you get squeamish at the thought of ripping your friend's heart out. Or perhaps you made the mistake of teaming up with a supervillain who is a ghost.* You may have to suck it up and take the coward's way out, which is fine. In fact, I have the utmost respect for cowards. Cowards are people who are *just smart*. When presented with situations that might mean an incredibly painful and squishy demise, they run away from them

---

* Listen, I have nothing against our ghost colleagues. They can be useful in all kinds of situations that require haunting or not touching things. But it's really hard to threaten them with anything but containment, and that's not nearly as fun as being able to say you're going to kick their spleens out. Bastards don't even have spleens. They've got ecto-spleens or something . . . that you can't kick.

instead of running towards them. That's simply common sense. Bravery is for suckers, and we'll let the superheroes keep that, thank you very much. I'm not sure why cowardice got such a bad rep . . . aren't cowards the survivors, after all? Anyway, I'm getting away from the point here. You can pretty much put an end to your own contract if you figure out a way to off yourself (don't worry, you'll come back . . . you always will), or conveniently make it look like you accidentally got eaten by that T. Rex you were planning to terrorize Venice Beach with. Lay low for a few months and everyone will be so busy with new stuff they probably won't even bring it up next time you cross paths at a meeting. These guys all have short memories.*

WORST PRACTICE IN ACTION:
Magneto and the Red Skull

Things weren't going so great in the Red Skull's Consortium of Masterminds, but they got even worse when Magneto, who spent time during his youth in a concentration camp, confronted the Skull about his time working with one Adolf Hitler. Skull said that it was all in the past, but Magneto wouldn't have it, so Skull tried to off the master of magnetism with some dust and scurried away. Magneto's a tough old villain, though. He tracked down the Skull (by bending some escape train tracks) and locked him up in an old fallout shelter to rot, with nothing but some water.

---

* Except for me. Pull that shit on me and I'll feed you to *six* T. Rexes!

Teaching Moment: When you're forming a team, it's smart to make sure you don't recruit anyone with a blood vendetta against you. If you have a blood vendetta against someone who has recruited you to a team (because you failed to take my advice, you ignorant pustule), going the "Cask of Amontillado" route is pretty clever. Poe's always a good resource.

Trick Everyone into Turning on Each Other

If you've set everything up correctly, this shouldn't be all that difficult to pull off. Just let the one member of the group who obeys your every word to tell another member that another member said he was going to be sure she doesn't get her share of the loot. That's basically the only seed you need to plant before everyone starts shooting beams at one another and the whole thing's down the crapper.

Create a Bigger Threat

If you can somehow distract everyone by creating a threat so huge that your team of villains has to team up with your sworn enemies—the heroes—to defeat you, the alliance is basically finito. So call up one of the space gods you know, ask them to alter reality so that everything is just slightly different, and then tell it to make everyone fight in a big war game or threaten to take a big dump on the planet. That ought to do it. And you've got some nigh-omnipotent space gods you can call up for favors, right? Sure. We all do.

Be Direct

Tell the group straight-up, "It's over. We're splitting." There will probably be a huge fight, and almost everyone will try to maul you for insisting that they won't get any of the loot or notoriety you spent weeks or months or years planning to obtain, but it'll give you the opportunity to feel like a really big deal for a couple hours, and what's the point of supervillainy if you can't feel like a King Shit every now and again?

Brainwash and Convince Them You are the Greatest Possible Threat to Their Safety

I know I keep going back to this well, but that's only because it's a plainly useful way to do things. It's just as convenient to have your fellow supervillains think you're a huge threat as it is to make superheroes or the general populaces feel the same way. A reputation as a destructive terror among your peers can yield big rewards and tons of respect. Buy up a lot of industrial-grade brainwash and keep it on-hand for basically any scenario. It'll come in so, so handy. (As dictated by the Metallica album title, *Master of Puppets*.)

Irreconcilable Differences: Publicizing the Divorce

One thing we like to say around the offices and death traps here at the ISS HQ is that nothing is really worth doing if you can't seize a few satellite dishes and radio antennas to announce it. That goes for your various and sundry announcements of how you're severing ties with your fellow super-villains just as much as it does proclaiming the city of Brussels is 98 percent liquid.

The thing is, it can be difficult to get the media—with their well-known hero bias—interested in the inside-baseball beltway politics of intravillain relations. All it takes is for a superhero to fart the wrong way toward another superhero and they're all over it like a toppling Saddam Hussein statue. Superheroes fight one another all the time, too; not so much because they dislike each other—like we do—but because they're always mistaking each other for supervillains, like it's anything but obvious that a guy in a big red cape or with tiny little wings on his temples is anything but a hero type. With us supervillains, we can straight-up strangle a dozen of our co-conspirators to death and grill their insides, and get little more than one line in the police blotter on page D7 of the *Shitburg Craprag*.

So if your breakup isn't going to set any reporters' hearts on fire, how can you ensure anyone pays attention? Try these techniques:

Threaten to Set a Reporter's Heart on Fire
That'll get those fourth estate rat-bastards' attention.

Do That Whole TV Network Takeover Thing I Mentioned Earlier
Just keep taking over the same one. They'll get used to you. Won't even put up a fight after a while. They may even take some initiative and tie themselves up.

Pull a Fake Face Turn

This isn't a well you can go to very often, but every once in a while it's likely to fool a rookie reporter or two. Announce that you're leaving your consortium of supervillainy because you've given up your life of crime—being around other supervillains has shown you how bad they truly are—and want to fight evil from now on (this is also a decent last-resort way to quit your team, though the other members may try to tie you to the fiery end of a rocket once you break the news to them, because it's in their natures). Like I said, superheroes get way more attention, so becoming one, even for a few days, and even if it's quite transparently a ploy to get noticed, will get you noticed. And as a bonus, you might even gain access to some idiot superhero's inner circle where you can steal some important secret information about them and all their friends' secret identities and whatnot.

Break up the Team in August

There's no news anyway in August.

Make It Political

If you can somehow frame the end of the partnership as some sort of political disagreement or scandal, or better yet, one of the members of your team holds some nominal elected office, you can surely get some story-hungry City Hall reporter to eat it up. Just use these key words: "back-biting," "greased palms," "Blagojevichy," "Petraeus," "backroom dealings," "redacted records," and "intel." Talk all kinds of talk about your special intel. Someone will bite.

Celebritize It

You're a supervillain. You're something of a celebrity. And you know what people love to read about celebrities doing? Getting divorced. So make your team breakup an actual romantic breakup. Marry one of the members of your squad, and then divorce them. The media may not give two shits about your business relationship shredding to pieces, but they can't get enough of horrible people's romances ending. Use it.

Chapter 6

Accusations

According to your thoughts, which I am looking over because I own them, most of you share the same number-one fear: Being brutally and painfully punished for your crimes for the rest of eternity in some sort of forever-torture chamber. I can tell you that those are indeed valid concerns. I personally have about eight forever-torture chambers here at the HQ, just in case one of you really, really pisses me off.*

But what you aren't taking into consideration is that that you may end up being pretty severely punished for something you never did at all. You're an evil person, that's the path you've chosen. (Though we've got some scientists working at ray gun-point on some break-throughs that are probably going to prove at there's an Evil Gene, so stay tuned on that!) Don't get me

Everybody wants to take a shot at you.

---

* I'm looking at you, guy, who keeps skipping around through the chapters. They're in this order for a reason, you uncultured *son of a bitch*.

wrong, virtually everyone else in the world has some level of evil in them, too, but they want to *believe* that they're good. So there's a reasonable chance you're going to get some undeserved fingers pointed your way during your career.

Say, for instance, that 12 million simoleons suddenly goes missing from the city treasury because the mayor wanted to take all twenty-four of his mistresses on a $500,000 vacation to Goldland (the area of Antarctica made of gold that only rich people know about). News gets out. If the mayor says all the stuff about him and his mistresses are fabrications, and, in fact, that supervillain lady who robbed $11 million from the treasury last year did it, who do you think people are going to believe?

Or, let's say a guy cuts the brakes on a subway train he knows his wife's going to be on so he can get her out of his hair and collect some sweet insurance money. But when he's on trial, he pawns the blame off on you, the Anti-Transit Man. That's not even kind of fair.

Supervillain FAQ: What media should I trust?

I have been talking quite a bit about the media and how you should distribute your various evil messages, and many of you have spent a lot of time thinking** about whether any particular news outfit is better suited to your purposes.

The short answer is no. Just about any media outlet is going to treat you the exact same way: They'll

---

** Reminder: I own your thoughts.

keep you at arm's length, as you're one of society's bad apples, but they'll also put anything and everything you do in their publication/program/blog/vlog/tweets, because people are fascinated by crazy weirdoes like you. As long as you know how to tantalize and keep them in the palm of your hand—it involves a lot of anonymous letters and very little outright begging for attention—they'll put anything you want said out there.

That said, it's still worth considering what type of news media is best for the particular types of evil missives you want to broadcast to the world. So here's a quick checklist:

Newspapers
Send messages to these when you wish to keep your appearance hidden, you have a complex message that won't come through well via broadcast media, or you need to speak directly and quickly to the very elderly. Take over when you need an editorial page in which to complain about local taxes.

Television
Perfect for when you want everyone to remember your face, your plan is simple enough to bark out in a ten-second sound bite, and you're being sponsored by a local furniture chain. Take these over when you've kidnapped the mayor and you need to prove it by tying him up to a giant prop Lincoln head or candy cane on a local game show set.

Radio
Use when your plan involves inane chatter about national celebrities and/or high school football. Take over these stations when your plan requires unlimited access to every Night Ranger song.

Blogs
Alert bloggers about what you're doing when you need a younger, in-the-know audience of about 100 people or less to know what you're up to. Take over a blog whenever your plan requires daily, emoticon-based updates regarding how you're feeling.

Online Video
For villains with cat-related or lip syncing powers only.

Social Media
Use when your master plan involves a change in your relationship status and is also only about two sentences long. Take over a social media site when you want to become the richest person on Earth, even though you make no actual money.

Books
Don't mess with books. I got books.

My point here is this: It sort of doesn't matter whether the accusations against you are *true*. People are going to be inclined to believe you did just about anything that's illegal or destructive or vindictive or costly, *even if it's impossible*, because as far as they know, you're basically responsible for everything bad that happens. And you know what? You can't really blame them. I mean, do blame them, because it's our job to blame everyone for everything that could even somewhat be perceived as a slight, but we've so far spent this entire book—or at least a big chunk of it—talking about how you can establish that very reputation. It only makes sense that you're going to pop into people's heads the second someone else's head explodes.

A lot of times, it's pretty awesome when you can take credit for nigh-impossible shit you didn't even do. But what you're looking for is credit, not blame. You want all the glory that comes with evil deeds you may or may not have done, but as soon as uniformed authority figures with restraining garments start approaching your lair gates about those things, it's time to get busy denyin'.

Fending Them Off

Lengthy trials and tribunals can be terribly time-consuming, and every second you spend in a courtroom is precious time you could be spending devising ways to set your arch-nemesis's bed sheets on fire. It's just wasted life . . . which is why it's important to try and clear your name. Again, whether you actually did the crime or not is irrelevant, just make sure you do it as quickly and simply as you can. Try these methods of making things easier for yourself:

Have a Well-Defined Gimmick

If you've got ice powers or a freeze ray, make sure everyone within your reach knows that's your deal. Put it in your name, like, if you're an older fellow, use Freezer Pop. I don't think that's taken. That way, when people in the town square are being burned with acid to the point of disfigurement, the coppers won't come calling for you (even if you, Freezer Pop, also have a thing for throwing acid at people).

Deflect

We supervillains aren't above pawning the blame for stuff off on our peers and colleagues. So do it. Point every finger you have at your similarly evil neighbor and skip town.

Blame it on Your (Even More) Evil Twin

Acquire a fake mustache (women, this can work for you, too), maybe some thick glasses, and voila! Suddenly, you are no longer yourself, but your heretofore never-before-seen sibling named, let's say, Fernando. The problem with this one, of course, is that you'll still have to attend court proceedings, just in the costume. Consider using a robot or something.

Blame Society

Okay, yes, maybe you did infect everyone at the opera with a virus that made them cry nonstop for an entire year. But the schools are really to blame for it! Or the superhero that punched you and damaged your brain! Or those video games and rap music!

Video games can also be effective.

Tamper with the Evidence

Is there video of you committing the crime? Edit it so that it looks like your superhero enemy is doing it. Eyewitnesses got you dead to rights? Erase their memories. Detectives found your prints at the scene? Get new hands. Police caught you right in the middle of the act? Sink the state.

WORST PRACTICE IN ACTION: Sinestro Blames His Future Crimes on the Tribunal

All it took for those ring-distributing space weirdoes in the Guardians to get all cheesed off at Sinestro was for him to conquer his home planet and rule over it as a dictator. Doesn't seem like that big of a deal to me, but the Guardians seemed to think it was a problem, so they banished the purple, mustachioed one to the antimatter universe. Sinestro didn't take the punishment lying down: He told the Guardians that any evil tendencies he gained while imprisoned was on them. Specifically, he said, "Whatever I become, you have made me!"

Teaching Moment: Anything that's "wrong" with you? That's just society, man. Society did this. Remember that.

Weathering Them

Sometimes, no matter how hard you try to avoid it, an allegation will stick and you'll have to simply deal with the consequences.* In particular, you'll have to make sure assertions that you committed crimes which don't fit with your established persona or performed actions (like laying blame

---

* More on evading the legal consequences of your actions in Chapter 7.

on someone else after you took credit for the deed) don't somehow weaken your personal brand.

If your brand is strong enough, then you can probably take the hit. But if you are only starting to get off the ground, you may need to take some fairly drastic steps. One thing you could do is have a henchman or clone start appearing everywhere as you for a couple weeks, then stage a very public and potentially embarrassing "death." Then, a few weeks later, make a triumphant return to the spotlight, announcing that the you which everyone had been seeing for the past few months—including when you supposedly did that thing that is not at all something you would ever do—was an impostor who obviously didn't know what they was doing.

Another thing you could do is claim your body had been temporarily overtaken by another supervillain's consciousness (or a bad writer whose work everyone should just ignore). That kind of garbage actually happens pretty often, so it won't be that hard for people to swallow.

Or you could sink the state and start over from scratch. Sometimes, no joke, you have to sink a state.

Turning the Tables

A moment ago, I mentioned the value of deflecting blame toward another supervillain. If there aren't any other supervillains around to throw under the bus (figuratively or literally), then you can always take the same approach to your accusers; be they superhero or regular old Joe Schmucko. But it's going to take a little bit of extra work to make sure a he said/supervillain said scenario turns out in your favor. For whatever reason, people are going to have a tendency not to believe your word against some "upstanding" citizen's, or a judge's, or even an orphan's. You're going to have to nudge it, thusly:

Start by maligning your accuser's character. Everyone's got something they don't want people knowing, and that can instantly ruin their credibility. The lucky-for-us part of this whole court of public opinion setup is that it doesn't even matter if your accuser's indiscretion is even anywhere close to the same league as yours. Let's say you're accused of turning a city block full of people into multicolored powder. All you have do is prove that the person accusing you cheated on his wife or slid by without paying his full income taxes one year. That's all you need! And if you're too busy coming up with your next plan to turn people into dust, you could always hire some patsy private eye. They're always patsies.

The even more direct route would be to simply fabricate something really weird or untrustworthy about your accuser, like you say maybe he or she likes to eat cats alive or ties people's shoelaces together or tosses babies around like footballs. It doesn't even have to make sense; just get it out there in the grapevine through some anonymous agents. Remember that it needs to look like it didn't come from you, and no matter how ludicrous it is, it'll put your target on the defensive and get TMZ talking.

Once the public's trust in your accuser is threatened, convince everyone that *they* actually did the crime. This maneuver, called the "smelt-it-dealt-it gambit," takes a little bit of finesse, but you can definitely pull it off. All you need is a hypnotism machine, some mind-altering chemicals, a time machine, a perfect doppelganger of your accuser or some combination of the four, and you can make your accuser the accused. What's good for the goose is good for the gander . . . that son-of-a-bitch gander.

All in the Shine: The Importance of Branding

Earlier, I mentioned how having a strong brand can be a big help in throwing the authorities off your scent when the crimes of the day don't fit your established gimmick. That's why Madame Caterpillar gets away with all those puma attacks.

But that's not all having a strong brand can get you. Allow me to share the following story of a villain whose odd, yet serendipitous name, led to infamy and notoriety beyond his wildest dreams.

Uh, hey. So, uh, my name is like, Come At Me Bro. I'm a supervillain. My power and stuff is that if, like, bros come at me, I can, like, stop them from coming at me. I'm really awesome at it. Like, I hold up my hand and they just stop. Then I can beat 'em up or whatever. I usually pick up and leave to go play some *Madden* with my brahs, though.

Anyway, I was this supervillain who nobody really knew very well for a few years. People thought my name was weird and stuff. They didn't get it. Superheroes got so confused by my name that they didn't even bother to come at me, bro! They just called their friends to try to understand what I was saying. It was pretty messed up.

It was cool, though, because a few years ago there was this thing on the Internet, you know, like a meme.** People would take pictures of cats or, like, He-Man, and put, 'Come at me bro' on them. I don't know if I started it somehow or what, but the pictures are all over the Internet now. You can search for them on Google. I'll show you on my phone right now, see?

Actually, I guess the reception's pretty bad down here. But you can look it up later. It's totally true.

So after that meme started, people started thinking I took my name from it or that I inspired it or whatever. I got phone calls to be on TV shows and stuff. Banks invited me to come rob them so the employees could all laugh about it on the Internet. Like, the Internet is funny, I guess. It felt kinda weird to do that, but they let me keep the money, so it's all good.

Now, I'm one of the most, like, popular and well-known supervillains. If people want to hire someone to come fight a superhero for them or whatever, a lot of them come to me because of that stuff from the Internet. People hire me

---

** Important Note: He pronounced it "mehm." He's a real piece of work, this guy.

for their business conferences and stuff. It's like pretty crazy and shit.

Hey, Mr. Oblivion? Dr. O? This room has been filling up with water for the past half hour or so. What's up with that? It's getting pretty close to my mouth and nose, dude. Can you maybe get a drain in here or something? That might be pretty cooggaggggagrarglr.

Kids sure do have some odd slang these days, don't they? Anyway, I hope you all took a valuable lesson from this: Pick a name that may become popular on the Internet someday, and people will *ask* you to come commit crimes for them. You won't have to earn it or anything! You can just be some young jerk who has everything handed to you.
I hope you learned.

Chapter 7

The Daring Escape

Jail time.
Imprisonment.
Incarceration.
A trip up the river.
A vacation to the crossbar hotel.
A visit to the house of numbers.
That period during which a lot of other
people of your same sex tried to have sex
with you in various ways, whether you
wanted them to or not.

Whatever you may call it, prison is an essential fact of life for the supervillain. Despite all your efforts to fend off every finger pointed your way, something is eventually gonna stick. Some jerkoff superhero is going to crash through one of your expensive windows and rat you out to the fuzz. Then a judge is going to make an example out of you, fast-tracking your case so that you make a hasty trip to a supermax. You may occasionally slip the noose by replacing your body with decoys or through sheer intimidation, but it's going to happen. You're going to go.

You have infinite ways to whittle away your time there: learning a new trade; reading every book in the library; building a ship in a bottle; learning to make wine out of urine; starting a social group or "gang," based on ethnicity and/or tattoos; trying to see how many other people you can shank in the stomach in a fifteen minute period; and working to improve your score each week.

Whatever you do to pass the time, you shouldn't spend too much of your downtime fitting in with the general population. Those peasants and layabouts are mostly decent people who got caught trying to sell some drugs or smothered their husbands in a crime of passion. They're not truly evil. Trying to build friendships or partnerships with them is like walking into your henchmen's quarters and asking them to play you in a game of rummy—a complete waste of time that probably would have been better spent trying to ferment pee.

The old ways don't work anymore.

As wonderful as the delights of piss-wine are, that really isn't the optimal use of your prison time either. At least, not all of it. As you indulge in the occasional sip of Peenot, you should be working day and night on your escape plan. Yes, it's true that you will most likely exit prison one way or another—supervillains get out, and that's the way it is—but that doesn't mean you don't have to put some effort into it. Who told you that it was okay to sit back and expect the prison doors to open up so you could just walk right out? I know you're thinking it. It wasn't me who told you, that much I know, you slovenly lump of purposeless cells.*

Supervillain FAQ: Should I pet a cat?

The classic James Bond villain, Ernst Stavro Blofeld, famously said, "Kill Bond! Now!" After which his cat said, "Mwrwaaarrarrrr!"

Because of classic moments like that, it's become a common trope for villains—especially those who go up against super spies—to constantly be accompanied by a feline companion. From Blofeld to Gargamel, to Dr. Evil to Dr. Claw, cats, particularly those with an affinity for bejeweled collars, have a long history in evil ventures.

But is it the best (worst) choice for you, the supervillain? You're no mere Bond villain (whom

---

* Okay, maybe it was me. In my other book, I may have said something about how you shouldn't worry, because you'll always get out of jail no problem. But you should know by now that *I am a liar*. You don't know what I'm gonna say! But trust me this time. You have to plan for your escape.

you should never mistake as "super"), but it could be a viable option. It depends.

First: How important are your hands?

A cat in your lap or in your arms means all the difference if your nemesis is the type who throws knuckles first and saves their clever quips for when you're in duress on the floor. It might be a good idea to have a pillow nearby, onto which you can throw your cat in case you need to quickly toss him or her aside. That, or you should be sure to have an endless supply of cats on hand, in case you accidentally keep throwing them into paper shredders or something.

Second: Scratches

They are going to happen.

Third: Do you mind looking kind of effeminate?

Don't worry if you do. For a lot of villains, that's their thing. It can work for you. If you're already a woman, this shouldn't be a problem at all, though you should be mindful of how people will perceive you if you have more than one cat on or around you.**

Fourth: Litter smell

You will smell like litter.

Fifth: How big is the cat?

If you're reaching up into leopard or even bobcat territory, you may be overreaching.

Finally: Consider what you're trying to say.

It could just be, "I like cats." But you're probably going to want to say more. Nothing else immediately comes to mind, though.

_____

** They will perceive you as a crazy person.

You've managed to disgust me so thoroughly that I feel like I shouldn't even bother to tell you all the different methods you can consider for your Earth-shattering escape plan, but I already set aside all this time to write this stuff out, and I really love to throw my weight around as an authority about these topics; so I guess I'll give you the benefit of the doubt, you lucky rat bastards.*

The Easy Ways

With access to the right equipment—conceivably brought in to the prison via a cake your henchmen baked for you— it's reasonably trouble-free to remove your shackles and step into the light as a free villain. The hard part, quite clearly, is getting your henchmen to bake anything convincingly, let alone a cake large enough to contain one of the very large and difficult-to-come-by apparatuses listed below. At the very least, tell them very early on in the process to bake the cake first, *then* insert the machine of your choice after the fact. There's not much good a baked time machine can do you.

Use a Time Machine

You can go back in time to before the prison was even there, move a mile or two in one direction, and then come back to your own time. Easy peasy. Be careful not to go back to saber-toothed tiger times, though. Those things were awful.†

---

* I'm not really giving you the benefit of the doubt. I just want to hear myself talk. Read myself write? You get the idea.

† If you're feeling particularly capable, you could try to capture one and make it your personal pet. More on pets at the end of this chapter.

Use a Reality-Altering Device

If uncertainty and fear regarding a savage past often creeps into your mind, skip the time travel and simply change the building you're in from a prison into, say, a Target. Then you can grab some snacks on the way out. But be careful to not to change the building into a lowercase-t target. Like, a nuclear test site. You could also use a reality alterer to simply make it so that the crime you committed never happened. Just make sure your *conviction* doesn't also happen.

Use a Memory Eraser

Erase everyone's memory of your crime and trial. Except mine, of course. I'm immune. I got all those thoughts stored up here in case I need them.

Use an Identity Switcher

If you're not all that invested in the face you have now, simply zap yourself with a handy-dandy device to change it, along with your DNA and fingerprints. Then the state won't have any choice other than to concede that you are not a person who has committed a crime and let you go.*

Use a Bulldozer

Not the most subtle approach; and it's really tough to fit one inside a cake, but is most effective.

---

* You should also make up a fake name in this scenario. I suggest Vincent von Innocent.

WORST PRACTICE IN ACTION:
The Kingpin Springs Himself

As rumors swirled that attorney Matt Murdock was, in fact, the superhero Daredevil, Wilson Fisk, a.k.a., the Kingpin, seized upon the moment. A prisoner at the time, Fisk offered the FBI special access to what he called the "Murdock Papers," which was smoking-gun proof that the famous blind lawyer was a superhero. Turns out there were no such papers, but Fisk got them proof of a sort as a result of the investigation. For cooperating, the feds let Fisk walk a free man (until they turned right around and arrested him again for a different crime).

Teaching Moment: Making shit up works.**

** Until it doesn't.

Higher Difficulty

Not all supervillains have access to high technology like memory erasers and bulldozers,* so they have to be a little bit more creative in how they go about removing themselves from their prison predicaments. If you are just such a supervillain, consider a plan of somewhat expedient escape such as one of these:

---

* If you're looking for some, though, I can set you up with a guy who can get some for you at a sweet price, only about 75 percent of which goes to me.

Warden-Rigging

With a series of increasingly urgent notes from the warden's "spouse," (which was written by you or one of your lackeys forging their handwriting, or maybe the warden's actual spouse, who you've kidnapped), convince the prison boss that they really ought to retire and get out of the whole jail business. Maybe they should consider opening a farm stand by the side of the road to sell dates or some such?* Once the warden inevitably announces their impending retirement, create a robotic version of or disguise a henchman as the next person in line for the job (it should be fairly obvious who's got their eyes on such a prominent position). Then, when that person is installed in the job, they can "acciden-tally" leave the door to your cell, block, and the prison itself open the next night, and you walk free.

The Pardon Switcheroo

Train one of your assistants/lackeys in the ways of politics (basic instruction: talk a lot about "issues" but really make everything personal) so that they can become the governor's chief of staff or secretary of butt shape or whatever they have these days. Then, have that assistant/lackey mention your name to the governor once an hour, every hour . . . even when the governor is sleeping. Make your name a word that the governor can't help but say without even meaning to say it. That way, when it comes time for the state's chief executive to issue his or her next pardon, you're sure to be the one to get that pardon, no matter whom the state executive meant to pardon. (Also, you're likely to get your name unwittingly

---

* All wardens secretly have a dream of starting up a roadside farm stand to sell dates or various other fruits.

put on any number of pieces of legislation, so prepare yourself for the Megaton Blast Master Anti-Gang Violence Act.)

Siege of the Walls

Rally your hench-troops to bombard the prison walls with whatever ordinance you may have available.* (Though, if you don't have a bulldozer, who knows what pittance of destruction that might be.) You should be aware that this technique is not designed to bust you out through force. The assault is merely a distraction to keep the guards and prison brass busy while you crawl through a tunnel you've been digging under your toilet for the past four months. If all goes right, you'll pop out next to a Target where you can buy some snacks.

Vampire Ambush

Make friends with some vampires before you go to prison. (Go to all the regular vampire hangouts, such as high schools and the woods.) Have them come bite everyone in the prison. Then the authorities will have more important things to worry about than keeping you in.

The "Legitimate" Way

If you have a top-notch attorney (and you should, I mean, come on, you're a supervillain), then their number-one job ought to be to make sure that, even if you're sentenced to 700 life sentences for sending an entire stadium of people into a black hole, you have at least some chance of parole. Parole is the lifeline of the supervillain who doesn't have a time machine or vampire friends or henchmen they can

---

* More about destructive tools in Chapter 10.

teach about government. It's pretty easy, too. All you have to do to is act as though you've reformed! Simply say, "I've learned my lesson and I want to go out into the world and do some good" at your hearing, and with the help of some basic hypnotism training or an attorney who can control minds (it really helps if your attorney can control minds), you'll be back out there sending whatever you please into black holes in no time.

Life of Riotly: When You're Incarcerated

Earlier, I made some facetious comments* about how drinking wine made out of pee in prison and people trying to have sex with you and reading books are things people actually do in prison.** But what is one really to do in jail when he or she isn't planning a route to the nearest place to buy snack foods? There are, in fact, lots of opportunities to learn some important stuff up in the hoosegow. Take advantage of it! You may never get the chance to learn these things again (though odds are you'll have dozens of jail trips over the decades to get to know this stuff).

Organizational Skills
It takes a lot of know-how to get twenty-five different people to gang up on the guy who looked

---

* Or maybe they were serious? Just trying to keep you on your toes.
** We all know the only good prison wine uses safe, pee-less toilet water.

at you funny in the cafeteria and stab him with a sharpened toothbrush. But if you build strong relationships with your inmates and can communicate clearly, you'll become a leader of those assorted ruffians. It's a project that you can make happen.

Self-Defense

If you aren't so great at building relationships with your fellow inmates and you accidentally look at one of the popular prison clique leaders funny in the cafeteria, seemingly everyone in there is going to try to stab you with a sharpened toothbrush. So it's pretty important that you learn judo or some type of hand-to-hand combat; either from the martial arts master they keep locked up on the top level of the prison (you have to fight your way up there) or, you know, just take a class sponsored by the community college.**

Crafts

You might think that you'll never use the toothbrush-sharpening skills outside prison, but you'd be surprised how far reinventing yourself as a supervillain with a stabby dentist shtick can take you. (Call yourself the Malicious Molar. You're welcome.)

The Art of Distraction

It's late at night. You remember that you left your best sharpened toothbrush out in the yard, and

---

** A full fighting style guide is available in Chapter 11.

you wrote down in your planner that you were going to get to stabbing your cellmate before breakfast. What to do? Only one thing to do! Get a riot going so you can slip out and go grab it before the guards tackle you and stick a billy club up your butthole. Frankly, it's pretty easy to start prison riots. All you really have to do is shout, "Your mom!" to no one in particular and you can get one going. But you'll learn some creative ways, too! Stuff like yelling, "Shut up!" or "How uncouth!"

Coded Language

It would be big trouble for you if a guard overheard you in the visiting room telling your top henchman to beat up and tie the superheroes they've apprehended to a couple of torpedoes so they can blast them out of a submarine into a colony of sharks. So you'll have to figure out some sort of code. "Oh, so you got the *hams*? Good work. Be sure to *tenderize them* for the *submarine sandwich* by tying them to some *torpedoes* and *shooting them* into a *colony of sharks*."

Advanced Egotism

Even if you work your way into a leadership position in the slammer, you'll come to discover—without much pushing—that the only person you can trust in there is yourself. As I said before, no one else in there is as evil and brilliant as you are.

Many of them are plain old idiots; people waiting out their time and thinking about how wrong they were to knock over that liquor store. You are not like them. You're already planning your next masterpiece. The one in which you'll replace the mayor with a living wax figure who looks just like him, and who'll name you city manager so you can repave the roads with poison-filled syringes. These people are worthless. They don't deserve to breathe the same air as you! Occupy the same space! What peons! What inconsequential ants! You hate them! You hate everything they stand for!

Thoughts like these will get you through prison, and you'll come out as big-headed as ever. Swell that head, supervillain! Swell it until it won't fit in the bars! (And consider recruiting those worthless idiots you're stuck in there with as henchmen—it's not like they're going to get hired anywhere else.)

Chapter 8

Acquiring Power

So, what are you in this for?

That sounds like an obvious question, and it is, though I don't need you sassing me about it, you pustule. I know your thoughts and don't appreciate them right now. And when I don't appreciate something, I often incinerate it, so FYI. Anyway, the question of why you got into this whole super-villain game is a pretty important one. It's so important that I dedicated two whole chapters to it in my previous book, which, I swear to God, if you've gotten this far into this book and haven't read the other one, you should mail me double the price and a written apology in hopes that I allow your nearest bookseller to provide you with a copy. (I own their thoughts, too.)

My point, and I do have one, is that most of us super-villains are looking for one of two or three things. Some, as Batman's butler pointed out in that horrible, propagandaish movie, just want to watch the world burn. Others have strictly pecuniary interests. But a good many of us supervillains—myself included—have ambitions beyond dancing on ashes or diving into giant piles of coins. We want to seize power. All the power.

Supervillain FAQ: Should I take drugs?

It's easy to think that, just because we supervillains do a lot of stuff that is illegal, we're supposed to do *everything* that's illegal. That's simply not so. For example, I have never driven drunk, because I've never driven, because I've always forced people to do that for me . . . often at ray gun-point. You can pick and choose the laws you want to break and obey the ones you like. It's not a full throttle shitting all over the law, it's more of a selective pissing on those parts that keep us from money or throwing cape-wearing individuals into open sewers.

So when you think about something like taking drugs, you need to consider more than just the fact that it's an illegal activity which much of the polite society looks down upon. You need to really think about whether the drug in question will actually make those illegal activities that are really important—the stuff about the money and the sewers— any easier. With that in mind, let's take a look at the pros and cons of some major ones, shall we?

Marijuana

Pros: Potentially relaxing after a long day of screaming death threats at henchmen; could help you make a breakthrough in your "hypnotize everyone with one incredible, really sweet tune" plan.

Cons: Demotivating; could inspire you to replace any plans you may have had with one that involves watching *Three's Company* reruns while you eat a whole thing of Danish sugar cookies.

Cocaine

Pros: Can really boost you through that frantic period of setting a takeover plan in motion; is a drug lots of business guys use, so will probably make you better at business.

Cons: Might make you jumpy, which may cause you to abort a plan prematurely or punch a mirror when you see your own masked reflection in it; could cause a stroke, and not one of the kinds that only makes you supervillain-appropriately disfigured.

Steroids

Pros: Will give you enough muscle power to give you a fighting chance against obnoxious superheroes; can increase aggression, which is a downside for most people, but should probably be a plus for someone who wants to go around throwing safes at people who pass by.

Cons: Testicular shrinkage or loss of femininity, and therefore wiles; won't do much good if the superhero you're fighting contains the power of 1,000 suns.

LSD
Pro: Opens pathways of perception to potentially free your mind to new ideas and avenues for villainous plans.

Con: Is hippie shit.

Methamphetamine
Pros: Again, can help you push through those long work nights; it can't hurt to jump on that already-diminishing *Breaking Bad* popularity bandwagon while you can.

Cons: Tooth loss could make all-important evil pronouncements more difficult to make; some other hot new TV show will showcase some other drug and then where will you be?

Opiates

Pros: Great for relieving pain in the aftermath of a superhero punching your jaw off or numbing you to it as it occurs; use of opium is known as "chasing the dragon," which means if you catch the dragon, maybe you can attack a city with it.

Cons: It's hard to conquer anything from the floor of a bathroom; all forms come from a flower, which isn't particularly evil on its face.

Ecstasy

Pro: The perfect thing to use if your plan involves dancing with glow sticks to house music.

Con: Useful for exactly no other purpose.

PCP

Pro: Can basically make you feel invincible, so you can charge right into a scuffle without fear.

Con: Does not hinder bullets or other objects from tearing through your skin and organs.

Alcohol

Pros: Can really get you in a fighting mood; helps loosen your lips if you're a shy type and need to give a big speech.

Cons: Slurred speech doesn't help much when you're trying to talk big; is legal, which I know I said wasn't a big deal earlier, but you have to admit it sort of removes the thrill of it all...

Nitrous oxide

Pros: Perfect for someone with an evil-medicine gimmick, and the mask looks appropriately nuts; makes you feel like laughing even when you don't want to, and laughing constantly is a pretty important supervillain trait.

Cons: Knocks you unconscious—more or less—which may not be the handiest thing when a being made of pure energy is coming toward you to kick you in the junk.

Nuke

Pro: Is such a powerful narcotic that it inspires cults around it and causes the streets to be overrun with crime in a manner never before seen.

Con: Does not exist yet. Society will have to wait until there are one or more RoboCops for it to go into production.

Of course, there isn't some infinite store of authority to go around. Some of us, that is, one of us (that is, me) operate on a global scale.* The rest of us, that is, the rest of you, have to aim smaller. Local.

---

* Though I'm looking to expand to the solar systemular scale very soon.

Taking over a small country or a municipality is a pretty big deal. It's not as easy as openly stomping into city hall and telling them to rewrite the charter so that it's nothing but your name. They make you stand in line and you have to sign in on a registry and then the mayor will make you wait for hours if they aren't out of town to begin with. If you go storming into a council meeting, they'll make you wait for a bunch of old ladies who are upset about a neighborhood bar being too rowdy before you can tell them all that you're going to melt them into their chairs. It's just not worth the hassle of dealing with the slow-turning wheels of local government. Not to mention that any local superheroes will probably stuff you into a trash can before you even get three steps inside the building. You'll have to find another way.

WORST PRACTICE IN ACTION: Two-Face Stakes His Claim

All it took for Two-Face to take over a big chunk of Gotham City was for a major earthquake to hit and for the federal government to shut off from the rest of the country. Thanks to those lucky breaks, old Harvey Dent kidnapped Police Commissioner James Gordon to ensure that his territory was secure. Other villains, such as Mr. Freeze and Penguin, had their own territory, but Two-Face really reached for the brass ring (until Lex Luthor showed up and spoiled the fun).

Teaching Moment: Sometimes you just have to let nature take its course. Then hope the government abandons all hope and leaves a big swath of your home city open for you to seize control.

Prep Work

For whatever reason, marching a huge force of henchmen into the town square to erect a 50-foot statue of yourself does not automatically make you the undisputed ruler of the land. It should almost certainly work that way, but people tend to have this weird attachment to what pieces of paper tell them instead of what giant slabs of granite tell them. So if you do that, it's likely the police, National Guard, or a mob of angered citizens will pull the thing down, as if you didn't force a team of minions to spend months of their precious time working on it.

This is especially true if no one knows who you are. As I have been saying throughout this book, name recognition is just as important to the power-hungry supervillain as intimidation skills and megalomaniacal tendencies . . . more so, really. Nobody's going to acknowledge your claim to their home as a real one if they think you're merely some weirdo off the street who happens to have working antennae attached to your head and an army of giant ants who follow you around.

So before you go putting busts of yourself all over town or unfurling banners with your face over every billboard, be sure to have these things lined up:

An Appropriate Target for Takeover

More on this in a bit.

A Reputation

I've been saying this since Chapter 1: You've got to have a killer rep. Since you're not actually in charge yet, one way you could build such a reputation is through a news report every week or so. These reports could simply consist of the anchors discussing amongst themselves what a bad influence you are on today's children, in that you are explicitly telling those children to beat up their parents with dowsing rods. You want the media to bring up your name with no real prompting. That's when you'll know you're a true threat.

An Army Entirely Loyal to You

Somebody's got to ward off the cops and local superheroes when they inevitably come after you the minute you've declared yourself leader of your new sovereign territory. Or, at least, someone's got to be around to herd them all into a mineshaft or onto a big boat so you can strand them, helpless, while you let anarchy reign for a few days. Alternately, you could simply take over the police force yourself using brain slugs. It's easier than you think to find brain slugs these days.

Collateral

People will be a lot more willing to accept you as their leader—or at least cede power over to you—if you hold their local professional football team captive and assure them they will be safe as long as they acknowledge your unyielding authority. You can always bank of people just loving the hell out of football.

A Sash or Hat That Says: "Leader"

Never doubt the hat or sash.

Say it, and they'll believe it.

A Direct Communications Link to the Public

Whether it's a citywide webcast that takes over every-one's computer or a signal takeover of every TV station in a 25-mile radius, you absolutely need to be able to talk to everyone in the area at once. Why? Read on.

Your Declaration

You've likely heard that the element of surprise is the key to gaining the upper hand against an enemy; and that's often the case. But when it comes to seizing control of a town, city, borough, unincorporated hamlet, tiny island nation, or whatever Cleveland is, a surprise attack just isn't the way to go. Again, no one's going to acknowledge your authority if they think you're a joke—an unhinged person with access to a particularly fancy cloak, when in fact you're an unhinged person with access to a particularly fancy cloak—a Napoleon complex and an occupying force in tow.

Your actions and the various news reports they engender will get that point across to the public to a degree, but you guys all know how I feel about getting your point across with nothing but actions. It's bullshit. So get on TV and say one or more or all of these things before you declare yourself the undisputed ruler of the land:

- "Prepare to be ruled."
- "Life as you know it is over. You will know prosperity under my leadership like you've never known before . . .

unless you cross me. That would mean you will experience much less prosperity. Unless you consider experiencing pain prospering. Then you'll be prosperous as hell."

- "Knock knock. Who's there? It's me, the person who rules you now. You were expecting a joke, I know."

- "I know you're probably scared. I would be, too. But look, could being frozen in a giant block of ice, which is what I plan to do to you, be any worse than your day jobs? Really think about that."

- "You may think I'm here to ruin your lives, but I'm really here to help you! I'm liberating you from the chains of money and possessions! First order of business: Give me all your money and possessions."

- "I'm not that bad of a person, really. Remind yourself of that as you spend the next decade of your life building a giant monument to me. Make sure my face looks right, but not *too* right."

- "You know where you are? You're in the jungle baby, you're gonna dieee."*

The Takeover

Once you've announced your plans to take over the position of king of the county, everything else should be relatively simple. March your henchmen around the city and get yourself an office; or maybe have them build you a castle. If the mayor's still around, put 'em in a glass box somewhere so that everyone can see that they've been neutralized. Put up

---

* This statement is the rightful copyright of Guns N' Roses and Geffen Records. Just be ready for the subpoena.

some billboards with your face on them! All people have to do is believe that you're the leader, and you are so.

Well, until *they* show up. But we'll get to them in a minute.

Might the Right Way: Choosing Your Target

What and whom, exactly, do you want to rule?

Lots of you are thinking that there's an obvious answer to that question, but the fact that each of you thought about different types of places right afterward proves to me that you're all idiots who need to stop thinking my rhetorical questions deserve responses from the likes of you. I'll train you yet!

Different people want different things. And, really, you'd better be glad about that . . . otherwise you'll never have the opportunity to rule anything. Some supervillain or scoundrel much more versed in the evil arts than you would have already claimed your dream kingdom for their own, and would thump you away like an ant.

Take me, for instance: I already have a vice grip of control on my home nation of Explosia, a grip I plan never to give up, even if the country's founder, Percival H. Exploso, walked out of his grave tomorrow. I'd as quickly drop him like a bag of dirt. Soon enough, I'll have the whole world, but you don't need to worry yourself about that right now. My point is, you're not getting Explosia.

Lucky for you, that's probably not a place you'd want to rule anyway. I know everyone who is from here and continues to live here, and none of them have any desire to wrest rule away from me, because I personally broke all their spirits. It's a hobby of mine.

What you need is your own Explosia. Consider these questions and you should arrive at that decision in no time.

How big should I go?

Neighborhood? Town? City? Small island nation? Something even bigger, like a planet in another dimension or solar system? You should scale your takeover plan according to your skills. If you're essentially what amounts to a low-level thug with some friends, stick to something small. A hamlet, maybe. If you have greater resources and some really cool powers, like, say, the ability to make buildings do whatever you tell them to, a decently-sized city should be well within reach. If you are really well organized and have some sort of floating fortress you can move around easily, then a small nation should be an appropriate goal. If you're a space god, go after other planets and dimensions. But don't come around here, big man. I've got cannons. Anti-space-god cannons.

Should it be my hometown/city/region/country?

This depends on one key factor: How much do you like your hometown? If you really love it, then why not take over your favorite place? If it's some-where you couldn't wait to escape as a kid, it's probably best not to spend all your time there as a conquering adult. But, if you hated every single person you knew there, you should probably go out of your way to make them suffer. Revenge feels terrific. Find that ex of yours and prove how much worse off they are because they dumped you by declaring that the only food available for their household are rusty nails. For extra theatricality, set it all up to coincide your ten-, twenty-, or thirty-year reunion! Reunite everyone under your iron fist.

What about the climate?
Are you a sentient being made of living fire? Consider a tropical area with some volcanoes. Are you so cold-hearted that you must constantly be in sub-zero temperatures to survive? Go for the poles. Are you a robot? Then you probably won't give a shit. Otherwise, stick to a temperate zone, you regular old flesh-person you.

Should it be a tourist spot?
On the one hand, it can be quite profitable to be in charge of a locale that attracts a lot of tourists. And, you know, it's more people to indenture into your servitude if you need the toilet fixed. But the thing about tourist destinations is that they have to be—and this is really a deal-breaker—appealing. It'll be harder to make your hell on earth a real hell-hole if you have to keep attracting families there.

Maybe if you took over Atlantic City, then nobody would notice.

Will I want to live there for the rest of my life?

You'd better want to. If you hate the beach, don't take over one of the Outer Banks. If you hate sentient rocks, don't take over Rockburg, the City of Rock People. These things should be no-brainers.

Do the people deserve my rule?

You don't want to control the lives of people who don't deserve your time and energy, do you? Study up on the schools, the median income, and the place's history. Are they a hardworking, hardy, self-sufficient people? Do the kids make good grades? Will their lack of appreciation of all the effort you put into crushing their little spirits be satisfying to you?

How difficult will it be to maintain power?

Are the people too smart? Too hardworking? Too self-sufficient? Will they almost certainly rise up and try to depose you by pelting your castle windows with the rudimentary tools you've given them to carve bas reliefs of your head? Then it may not be worth it, pal.

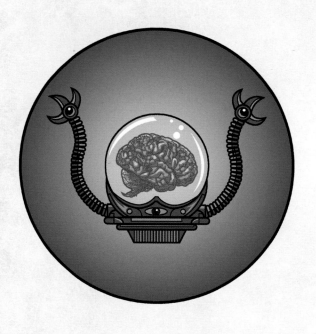

Chapter 9

Wielding Power

Congratulations! You have successfully wrested power away from the leadership of a territory, municipality, or other such fiefdom and claimed it as your own. Get a crown made. Buy a throne. Go nuts. But do not, and I mean do not, let your guard down.

You've got to look the part.

As Shakespeare sort of wrote in *Henry IV*, "Heavy is the head that wears the crown."* He was right. Jewels and shit are heavy. I wear that stuff all the time and if it weren't for my sincerely champion-like neck, I'd probably have a lot of difficulty with that. But you know the real reason why that head is so heavy? Because it's grown. And that's not just from the healthy ego boost a daring conqueror attains from becoming a ruler. It's also from all the targets people have attached directly to it.

Supervillain FAQ: Where should I get my clothes?

"The clothes make the man."
—someone who didn't under-
stand how
reproduction works.

Even though that fatuous fool was wrong, clothes are a huge part of someone's persona. You'd know that if you read *The Supervillain Handbook* as many times as you should have.** That's especially true of the worldly, accomplished people who become supervillains. Magneto and Darkseid don't exactly buy their threads off the rack at

** At least a dozen times. One dozen!

* The actual text of the play says, "Uneasy lies the head that wears the crown," but what am I, the quote police? If anything, I should be adding other extra words to make it more incorrect. "Heavy is the heart that does the shit." There.

T.J.Maxx. So where do they get them? In a few different places.

Pick the attire acquire method that's right for you:

Get a Personal Tailor

Many supervillains kidnap and indenture tailors rather early on in their evil careers; making them sort of like henchmen, but for clothes. Where can you find these tailors? I don't know, tailor schools? The yellow pages? Probably lots of places. I'm not your mom. Figure it out.

Do It Yourself

Nobody knows exactly what you need better than you. So if you're someone who can, say, control plants—like Poison Ivy does—just make your clothes out of your plants! Then your boobs can pop out and distract the superhero the exact amount that you want them to.

Get an Outfit Magicked Up

You probably know some magic people. Tell them to magic you up something nice, and *not to curse it*.**

Earn Them

Many fight-to-the-death contests in the far corners of space feature a grand prize of an ancient suit of alien armor. So step up, beat a 400-foot-tall

----

** That last part's pretty important.

immortal being made of black holes in combat, and it's yours!

Have a Giant Multinational Corporation's Resources Available

How do you think Luthor got that purple and green monstrosity he wears around? By having employees who can't tell him "no," that's how.

Have Some Armor Forged

Forges and blacksmiths are a little harder to come by today than they used to be, but I bet you can find one somewhere. Again, it's not my job to find these people for you.

Steal Them

How did this not already occur to you? Where is your head?

Kill an Ancient or Mystical Animal and Wear its Skin

Or you could just stomp on a few raccoons and tell everyone that they were mystical. Nobody'll know the difference.

Make the Clothes a Permanent Part of Your Body

I think that's how Bizarro's clothes work. Isn't it? Somebody call Bizarro and ask him. You know what, on second thought, nobody talk to Bizarro. He will not let up for hours if he gets a hold of your ear, no joke.

Everyone is going to be gunning for you. The people of the land, many of whom may think they liked things better before you mandated 120 percent of their income be sent to you in a daily pay-me tax enforced by robot visits to their door every hour, on the hour. The leaders of surrounding areas, who maybe had friendly diplomatic relations with the last administration, only for you to send dozens of ray gun-toting thugs into their warehouses to steal their meat, vegetables, and sugar.* The government and army of the country of which the city you have taken over used to be a part. You'll also have to deal with other supervillains, who may try to swoop in and pull the same hijinks you just did. It's a long list.

With all that unwanted attention focused upon you virtually all day, every day, you'll quickly learn that the main goal of your tenure as the unquestioned leader of your kingdom will be to extend and continue your tenure as the unquestioned leader of your kingdom. Part of that is pretty intuitive: defense, defense, defense. The other part is something that doesn't come quite so easily to us supervillains: Actually trying to make people less miserable.

Protective Measures

If you did things the proper way and followed my instructions from the last chapter, then you should have a well-sized cadre of henchmen at your disposal to serve as a barrier between you and anyone who might want to come at the king.† But you should take some additional actions once

---

* You closed all the farms because farms are boring.
† Actually, you know what? Don't use the word "king." That's my thing, and I feel like I've kind of got a brand going with that. You could be a baron. Or a duke. Oh, how about an earl! I bet you'd be a great earl.

you've actually cemented your position as leader for some extra insurance. Do all or most of these things, or you might as well take all the giant oil paintings of your head you were planning to wallpaper all the government buildings with and throw them in the middle of a lake . . . of lava.

Destroy Bridges and Tunnels

Seal off the city. Otherwise you'll get all kinds of military types and attack forces; an egress of people trying to flee you in terror. Yes, this means all the food you'll have will be well out of date within a short few months and become potentially deadly. But that's a small price to pay. (For you, personally, have some food flown in.)

Place a Dome over the City

Attack forces also have planes and helicopters and pigeon missiles.* Shut that down right away. Dome the city and keep them out. *But, King O.*, you're now all simultaneously thinking, *what about the food you mentioned just a minute ago?* Have an entry bubble that's protected with a very difficult-to-decipher password. Something like "ENTRY," or your name. Real head scratchers.

---

* Missiles made out of pigeons. They're horrifying. Trust me, I invented them.

Cannons

It's always prudent to have a few cannons around.

Dispose of the Dissidents

You'll know after a very short period of rule which citizens are the real shit-stirrers. Round those people up, put them on trial in a kangaroo court (if you feel it necessary to have a court at all), and exile them to the bottom of that lake of lava I mentioned a second ago.

Wipe Yourself off the Map

You know how to really stop people from bothering you? Make it so they don't know you're there! On how many maps have you seen Explosia? I'll tell you: Zero. That's because I bribed, threatened, and replaced every mapmaker in the world to keep it off there. Rand McNally has nightmares about me. Sure, it makes it harder to find the closest Arby's on your smartphone when you get a hankering for some curly fries, but when you're the ruler, you can put an Arby's in your house. Why the hell not? (Just be sure to have food flown in for them to use.)

Go Underground

If the forces amassed against you somehow manage to get through your dome or rebuild a bridge you destroyed or even dodge all your cannonballs, they still won't be able to dispose of you if they can't find you. Build yourself a bunker in an undisclosed location several miles below or outside of the city limits. No one will be the wiser.*

---

* Unless they read this, which competing supervillains almost certainly will do. If one of those guys is after you, live in a hot air balloon.

WORST PRACTICE IN ACTION: Ultron Takes Control of Slorenia

Evil, genocidal robot Ultron made it easy for himself when he decided to seize control of the tiny Eastern European nation of Slorenia. He up and killed everybody.

Teaching moment: It may be less of an accomplishment if you have no one to rule over, but taking the Ultron route will certainly mean you are a *definitive* ruler. You've just got to work out what you want more.**

** Which I'll be discussing further in the next chapter.

Bread and Circuses

Roman emperors had some really compelling ideas. I mean, a whole bunch of them. For instance, Nero and Caligula were basically proto-supervillains, though Caligula maybe even went beyond behavior even we can condone. The idea that applies to what we're talking about here is the notion of "bread and circuses"; the idea that keeping people appeased, entertained, and fat will stop them from dissenting. Take a page from their book with these activities in the place you rule:

Gladiatorial Fights to the Death

Since the Romans had such great ideas, why not take a page directly from their playbook? People love to see other people who aren't them torn apart by lions or forced to fight each other until one has the other on the ground, ready to have his or her throat sliced as you make the mortal decision for them. . . . Just as long as they know it'll never happen to them. So it's probably best you don't tell your subjects that they're all in the pool for the random drawings.

Free Continental Breakfast Once a Month

I know. Cereal and eggs can be expensive. But it's worth the cost once every thirty days to put down any insurgency. Plus, you can lace the coffee with sedatives so that no one gets too uprisy. Put enough in there and you could make them pretty damn downrisy.

Holidays in Your Honor

When folks have lives of intense and seemingly unending menial labor—which is what you're going to have most of your subjects doing here—they start to appreciate really minor things; like single days off. . . . Even if those days are dedicated to exchanging cards with your face on them and purchasing gifts for you. Have one every few weeks, and be sure to make wish lists. If you don't ask for 1,000 Keurig machines you won't get 1,000 Keurig machines.

Biographical Films in the Park

A thriving art community is very important to people. You should allow any budding filmmakers under your rule to make any film he or she wants . . . as long as it's a glowing piece of propaganda about your life. Then you can herd people into the park (or the gladiatorial arena) for mandatory movie nights! It'll be fun!

The "Internet"

Your people will want to feel connected to the world at large. Don't cut them completely off! Make sure all your computational machines in homes and libraries have access to a <u>handful</u> of Internet websites (literally five): The ISS website, WebMD (this way you won't need to license any doctors), a news website you create,* your Wikipedia page (only the version in the document history you approve and/or wrote, though), and Facebook (but they can only friend their mothers and high school friends who now have annoying opinions they express constantly; this will be a punishment).

---

* See Fox News as a jumping off point.

The Sympathy Card

There may come a time . . . actually, let me correct myself*; there almost certainly will come a time when you are on the ropes. Military or other authorities will break through your defenses and will try to convince your people that they should follow someone who isn't you. Your henchmen can fend them off for a while, but you can't keep that going forever. So what do you do? Something no supervillain ever wants to consider doing: Relying on the kindness of others.

The thing that ultimately gives a leader power is the consent of the people. Of course, I just spent two chapters talking about how to coerce unconsenting people into following you. But maybe, if you last long enough, people will get use to you that they will want you to stay in charge. Even if the situation they're in is awful, people tend to find change distasteful and scary . . . which is why they'll defend you if you keep them under your thumb long enough. It's sort of like collective Stockholm Syndrome. I call it, Latveria Syndrome.

Last as long as you can and make it happen.†

One Final Warning

If you somehow convince the people you rule to like you, be careful not to lose your edge. The last thing you want to become, through some process of bonding with your subjects and learning to love them as they have you, is a benevolent master. If you have to, bring in a few busloads of

---

* Not that I need to, right? Say it out loud, "Not that you need to, King."
† You may think this sentence is an opportunity for me to make a crack about sex. But lasting as long as you can at sex is terrible advice, for men and women. You're a supervillain! Your time is at a premium! Knock that shit out and get down to business!

new subjects every couple months to remind yourself you're a terrible human being.

Whatever it takes to ensure you don't slip out of your groove and lose your dominance.*

Trust, but Don't Really Trust: Choosing Your Advisors

If you recall from the chapters on alliances (and I know you don't; I can see from your thoughts that your reading comprehension is just atrocious, which is why I have to keep reminding you of things like this, which means you are personally wasting my time), trust is not a common attribute among supervillains. Nor should it be. The only person you can really trust, ever, is yourself . . . and sometimes, even you can pull some mightily diabolical tricks on various versions of yourself, past, present, and alternate dimension.*

And yet, it's entirely necessary to select a council of ministers** to sit around a table and offer you advice. Why? Because what use is being

---

* If you ever encounter a guy named Tyrannus Eradico, that's a version of me from the future who's trying to kill me. Give that guy an uppercut directly to the taint.

** And do call them ministers. "Secretary" just does not sound nefarious enough, no matter how you say it.

---

* This, however, is pretty good sex advice.

a leader if you don't have a group of people to sit around a conference table and order around? That would be completely worthless.

So keep in mind that everyone who sits around that table would love to depose and kill you. Use every trick in the book (this one) to ensure you come out on top of the sure-to-be-short-lived cabinet. Also, in case you're asking how a cabinet is different from an alliance, remember that alliances try to gain money or power, and cabinets try to retain or make more of it. There's less of a need here to assert your authority; you have already proven that. I mean, your face is carved into the Chamber of Pain, formerly known as City Hall.

Now that we have that out of the way, what sorts of advisors will you need? You'll need quite a few to fill out some necessary offices that you're sort of required to call the opposite of what they really are. To help you get a feel for this, I'll clue you in to who sits on my current cabinet before I throw them all in an incinerator next month:

Minister of Information (lying)

This should be someone who sounds like they know what they're talking about on any topic, even though you never actually tell them any of your plans or policies.

My Minister: Confuse-cious, who talks in nothing but wise-sounding aphorisms that, in reality, slowly destroy your brain.

Minister of Safety (beating up old ladies and children)

Make this someone with incredibly large muscles.

<u>My Minister</u>: The Bicep. He's 77 percent bicep!

Minister of Commerce (stealing things)

You can choose an out-and-out thief for this office, or you could make it someone who specializes in strong-arming store owners for protection money. Either way, you're going to need a second thief/extortionist to get your money away from *them*.

<u>My Minister</u>: Thief Thief, the thief who steals from thieves. (My secondary minister is Thief Thief Thief.)

Minister of Transportation (making sure no one goes anywhere)

This is the spot for a demolition expert, or, as I mentioned previously, someone who owns a giant dome.

<u>My Minister</u>: Serena Shapeshift. Right now, she *is* the dome.

Minister of the Interior (putting your face on everything)

Find an artistic supervillain to do this for you. Someone who can add a little pizzazz to your goofy mug.

<u>My Minister</u>: Banksy. That's right, I got Banksy.

Minister of Agriculture (barely adequate food)

This can be anybody, really. They don't have to do much of anything; just sit around and hold an office. It can be a brain in a jar. What do you care?

<u>My Minister</u>: Brain in a Jar III, grandson of the original Brain in a Jar.

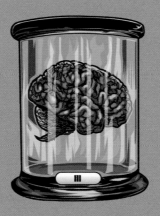

Minister of Labor (okay, this title is pretty accurate)

Pick someone who can really get workers motivated. And by "motivated," I mean that they can threaten them with nose, ear, and throat loss if they don't work on what you tell them to.

<u>My Minister</u>: Chillary Clintomb, a clone of Hillary Clinton, who is a tiny, little bit meaner version.

Minister of Finance (printing worthless money with your picture on it)

You need a numbers expert here, so consider reanimating Gottfried Leibniz, Isaac Newton, or the guy who invented the abacus and dosing them with insanity juice. Easy enough.

<u>My Minister</u>: Reanimated Isaac Newton, so you actually can't have him.

Minister of Education (brainwashing)

A hypnotist. Or maybe a person made out of brain detergent. This isn't that hard to work out.

<u>My Minister</u>: Spiralia, the human hypnosis spiral.

Minister of Peace (attacking anything that comes within 50 feet of you)

This should be someone who can see every angle. A tactician. A really strategically-minded person. (But don't go nuts, or they'll cut your legs off before you can blink and grab up your throne.)

<u>My Minister</u>: Aztec god of war, sacrifice, and sun, Huitzilopochtli. I give him a human heart every now and again, and that seems to satisfy him.**

** Full disclosure: He does creep me out a little.

Chapter 10

Preparing for Destruction

If you're the type of supervillain who eschews control and prefers to cause wanton chaos by making things explode, then you should know that you're merely doing the work of nature itself. As Marquis de Sade—a man who we should all model some aspects of our life after—once said, "Destruction, hence, like creation, is one of Nature's mandates."

A crazy French nobleman who liked to poison prostitutes said it, so therefore it must be true.

The crack of doom is as much a part of human life on Earth as the crack of dawn. To create devastation is simply to be of the world. But just because something is natural doesn't mean it's instinctive. Much like conquering, destroying—if it is to be done properly—is something you must plan, prepare, and gird yourself for. Rolling into town and immediately shooting rockets at train trestles, flipping cars onto their roofs, or eating your way through the artifacts in a museum may be a lot of fun, but it won't last for very long if you don't meticulously set your warpath and devise your methods for cutting through that path in a thoughtful and deliberate way.

This concept is often more difficult for the explodey types to wrap their heads around than it is for the wannabe dictators. Leadership candidates love planning and machinations and all that shit; it's sort of what they live for. So

Ray guns don't need cocking, but get some slides installed on yours anyway. It looks cool.

when you tell them it takes months—if not years—of agonizing forethought to achieve their goals, they pretty much follow you every step of the way.* The real psychopaths, the ones who want little more than to watch mountains get leveled, tend to lack patience. Why sit around putting little dots on maps when you could be putting huge dots on real landmarks in the form of craters?

Here's why: You need to make a statement if you really want to make a name for yourself. And everyone does, even those of us most single-mindedly obsessed with melting

---

* This, despite the fact that they're supposed to be leaders. Just between us, they're sheep. I'm assuming they're not reading this chapter. If you are a to-be leader and you're reading this, I'm not talking about you! Do everything I say.

hospitals. So you've got to make your annihilation *say* something about you, about society, about what you think of McDonalds taking your favorite sandwich off the dollar menu; whatever is most pressing to you at the moment. More on this in at the end of the chapter, when you're more willing to listen to me, you impatient, obstinate, lunkhead.

Supervillain FAQ: Is it okay to have kids?

It's so easy for us supervillains to get caught up in the day-to-day of evil, the destruction of lives, that some of us don't even think too much about the act of creating life. And I don't mean making clones of yourself or bizarro versions of superheroes in big tubes from your space lab, even though copying is creation of a sort. No, I mean making babies.

It's also easy to write off having children as a needless distraction; a responsibility that will remove you from the more important work of throwing an entire city's keys in the ocean. But there are big upsides to it, even beyond having a person that is an enduring part of yourself that will live on beyond your years and that even your shriveled heart can feel something for.**

Beyond that, it can sneak up on you. You go out to the local dastard bar, drink yourself silly, and a few months later, you've got a bastard

---

** Not that I would know. I'd never know anything about that.

dastard. Before you jump into a time machine and stop yourself, you may want to think over these pros and cons:

Pro: Something in your life to take your mind off of incredible stresses.

Con: An incredible stressor that keeps you from dealing with that other stuff—evil plans— and which therefore makes you incredibly stressed.

Pro: Free labor, at least for a few years, anyway.

Con: Labor of the quality a child would perform, because it's being performed by a child.**

Pro: While others can only give you their word in regards to loyalty, your child is your blood.

Con: Children are often very rebellious, which in your case means they'll probably join the Peace Corps or, worse, go into heroing; at least during those volatile teen years.

Pro: Someone else to blame in case things don't go the way you planned.

Con: Certain to be a constant disappointment because of you blaming things on them.

Pro: Can carry on your legacy after you have died or when you're serving a stint in prison.

** Not much worse than henchmen, though.

Con: May have plans different from your very specific ones for your long-lasting legacy; might try to take whatever you had planned and make it "hip."

Pro: Is a little you.
Con: Is a little you.

Let me appeal to your inherent impetuousness and/or laziness with this additional point: Planning and preparation actually make destruction *easier*. It may be hard to believe that laying groundwork is really the path of least resistance, but *consider whose book you're reading and maybe have a little damn respect*. Also, remember this statement: Make it your mantra.

The Most Effective Chaos Causes Itself

That may be a little too poetic to clear your lead-lined skulls, so I'll clarify. You can destroy a car at a time if you go out and run around a parking lot, flipping them over. But what if *extremely panicked people* were driving those cars? A bunch would probably get completely trashed *on their own* without you having to flip a single car. Or consider this scenario: You could walk into a bank with a disintegrating ray and aim it at individual people, who will probably be scared. Or you could toss a disintegrating grenade in there and freak everyone out at once.

I know it can feel a little disappointing to know that you can actually do more damage with a hands-off approach than one which involves you carrying around an enchanted flamethrower, but you can get involved with the flambé party once you really set the stage for it.

How do you set the stage? Like this:

Start with Talk

This is part of the ongoing theme I've been talking about throughout this guide: Sometimes, words are the most powerful weapon you have. Making all the mailboxes around the city come to life and eat people or infusing all the water with deadly high-fructose corn syrup or even lacing dollar bills with a drug that makes everyone's hair fall out can really cause a lot of havoc; but you know what would make things even more chaotic? A really vague threat, issued to everyone via a giant TV in the public square. "Need to send a letter? The box may request additional postage!" you might say. Or "We'd all like a little extra cash. Why not go take a few bucks out of the ATM right now? You'll only regret it . . . later."

Why these more cryptic, riddlesque statements instead of more direct threats? For one thing, directness is no real fun. Forthrightness is simply not supervillainous. More importantly, what you want to inspire, in addition to fear, is curiosity. People will certainly be scared by anything you say, especially if you've built yourself a worthwhile, terrifying, "insomniac name" reputation. But if you make your pronouncement vague enough, you'll also get people wondering, "Just what the hell was that masked psychopath talking about? I feel this weird urge to know!"

That's when people, entirely against their better judgment, will drink that diabetes water or go take out that alopecia cash. They'll lead themselves to their own downfall.

Plan for a Long Game

It's difficult for supervillains with destructive personalities to get involved in protracted scheming, but consider how much more you can do with a series of concentrated events throughout a series of weeks or months:

- A stadium turned into liquid here;
- A museum filled with gas that makes people intangible there;
- A portal opening up so a dinosaur can come through and trample a thousand cars over yon.

This could, bit by bit, whittle down the human spirit. A rush of carnage can do a lot of damage in a short period, but when it's over, it's over, and people go back to their lives. Spread it out, and you'll find the fruit of destruction well-ripened for the picking when you finally do unleash the final barrage.

The Calm Before the Swarm

Once you have warned everyone that something is coming, just lay fallow for a while. Don't do anything. Stay at home and make some pottery. Let them stew in it for a few days. Be quiet . . . too quiet. The collective freakout will reach immense proportions. Don't wait too long, though. You don't want people forgetting. Collectiblast waited three years once and his pog-themed trap backfired on him.

Gain Some Trust

The old "I'm reformed, honest!" gambit can really work to your advantage. If people are stupid enough to believe that you, a known criminal, have given up wanting to melt humans all of a sudden, they'll also be stupid enough to give you access to places they almost certainly should not. Take advantage! Get yourself into sensitive areas so you can better poke them. The one downside is you can probably only pull this off once.*

WORST PRACTICE IN ACTION: Darkseid Comes to Earth

Darkseid really plans ahead. When his son, Orion, "killed" him by ripping his heart out, evil New God sent his spirit back in time to inhabit the body of a human. He then had his servant, Libra, indoctrinate hundreds of supervillains and get them to join his service. Through that pre-planning, Darkseid actually conquered Earth and damn near destroyed it, but Batman shot him with a radion bullet and Superman sang into a machine and everything went back to the way it was. But at least Batman had to go spiraling through time after that.

Teaching Moment: If you can control what vessels your spirit inhabits and hire people with Svengali-like persuasion powers, do it. You'll get a lot more destroying done.

---

* And if you already did it to get out of an alliance—as I mentioned in Chapter 5—or to get some media attention—as I said in Chapter 6 (what can I say, a lot of recipes have the same ingredients)—you've probably used your one get-out-of-jail-free card. You'll have to land on Chance—a plastic surgeon's office—to get another one.

Amassing Your Arsenal

In *The Supervillain Handbook*, I spoke about the importance of the various ray guns you may wish to use. And indeed, ray guns are the bread and butter of things supervillains use to zap people. But to only use ray guns is to limit yourself, like a chef who has a kitchen full of utensils, but only uses ladles.* You need to expand your horizons, particularly if you want to do mass villainous destruction. Rays are great for scalpel-like precision, but sometimes, you really have to go big.

With that in mind, here are many of the tools available to you, and what they're best for:

Plasma Cannons

Remember what I said earlier about how it's always smart to have cannons? These shoot plasma. They're the logical next step from ray guns.

Portals

It's not so much the portals that are your weapons as what you can send through them: Alien squid monsters, omnipotent beings from other dimensions, the Justin Bieber album from the 2040s that will make everyone in the future hopelessly insane. So many options.

---

* Ladles are the bread and butter of kitchen utensils.

Gases

For knocking people out ,making them laugh themselves to death, or simply making it hard to see. Gases are extremely versatile.

Acid

If you really want to mess up a face, it's hard to compete with acid.

Bombs

You can go with the conventional, fiery type, or you can go with the kinds that beam death light everywhere or send anyone they blast spiraling through history. You can't go wrong with whatever you choose.

Lasers from Space

Lasers are way more fun when they are shot from space. That is a fact.

Giant Animals of Various Species

Sometimes a little bit hard to control, but you always get a lot of bang for your buck with these. I'd suggest keeping away from fish or birds, though. Stick to lizards, dinosaurs, apes/gorillas, bugs, horrifying mythical creatures, and so on.

Robots

Robots are like henchmen, except you can make their arms ray guns.

Or you can make them walking bombs.

Or you can make them gigantic and have them terrorize the city like a big ape would, without all the control problems! Robots are really an excellent choice.

Nanobots

Like robots, but tinier. You can have them do all the stuff robots can do; just on a smaller scale. Instead of knocking down your enemies or buildings, they can knock down someone's pancreas. And sometimes, you just need that.

Celestial Objects

Nothing like a comet or a meteor to really leave a crater worth writing home about.

Mind Barbs

These are barbs you shoot with your mind. Super-effective.

Demons/Hellfire

Again, you'll likely encounter some serious control issues with these, but nothing and no one does chaos better than demons shooting fire from hell. They always get the job done.

Doomsday Devices

These intentionally vague devices do what they say they'll do: They end the world. This is why it's preferable to only use these as a threat, rather than as an actionable weapon. Some of us want to rule stuff, so have some consideration.

Communication Through Kabooms: Saying Something With Your Wrath

As I mentioned prior to my lengthy argument convincing you that patience can actually get you somewhere—you brusque, uncivilized animal—I mentioned how important it is to really get a message across with your slings and volleys. Wanton and careless destruction is fun while it lasts, but unless you really attach a lasting, personal meaning to it, it will be forgotten as soon as your victims rebuild their bridges or come to terms with the fact that their Uncle Willis is made of sand now.

Now, that doesn't mean you have to, for example, spell out your name with big fiery letters across a city street or re-sculpt all the statues in Rome so that all the faces are yours. You can take a more subtle approach. If and when your rampage is documented in those propaganda rags called comic books, someone is going to have to characterize the sounds of your fury with words. Onomatopoeias. And though they may simply seem like words that represent sounds, they also all send slightly different signals about just who made them.

So know what you're saying. Here are a handful of common examples, and what you're saying when you make them happen:

BOOM: "I'm a straightforward person with an explosive personality. I hate frills, which makes me a pretty weak supervillain, to be totally honest."

KABOOM: "I have an explosive personality, but I don't mind frills at all. Frills like the letters 'K' and 'A.'"

BADOOM: "I have an explosive personality, and am bad. And like doom. I am multifaceted."

BOOM-SHAKA-LAKA: "No one can compete with the intensity of my dunks."

WHAM: "I speak with my fists. Also, I'm never gonna dance again."

FWOMP: "I let my body and its massive girth do the talking for me. This is because I get tired from opening my mouth."

KRAKADOOM: "I control the very lightning and thunder itself! Potentially, I also love crack."

BADOOSH: "I am a bad douche."

KRRRSHH: "I hate glass! Glass can eat me."

KRAK-OW: "My hits are so furious that they have two syllables. Additionally, I lack any sensitivity toward folks with Polish heritage."

KA-CHUNK: "I am a decapitator. The chunk I have ka-ed is your head."

WUSHHHH: "Floods are my thing. Some of Old Testament God's ideas were gems."

FAWOOSH: "I am a firestarter. Yes, yes, like the guy from that '90s song."

RAT-A-TAT-TAT: "I keep my distance and use guns, though preferably none made after 1945."

BUDDA-BUDDA-BUDDA: "I use more modern weaponry and lack any sensitivity to members of a particular religious group."

KRK-KRK-KRK: "I am as cool as ice; therefore I use it to destroy. Yes, yes, like that guy from that '90s song."

SHINK: "A recluse; I use stealth and blades to do damage. I shun attention, which makes me a very weak supervillain."

SKRRRRCH: "I rip my victims to pieces! It also helps if my victims are made of paper."

SQUITCCCH: "I like things messy, which is why I'm eating this meatball sub while I stomp in your ribs."

ZZZZZKK: "Electrical power courses through my body! I am in constant pain!"

HRRRKK: "I am in constant pain, but electrical power does not course through my body."

HRONK: "I attack with the fierceness of a rhinoceros or possibly a whooping crane."

SKRONCH: "I can crush people like I would an aluminum can! I also crush a lot of aluminum cans!"

SWOOSH: "I have no regard whatsoever for Nike's long-standing trademark!"

PING PING PING: "I am Darkseid or I wish to be destroyed by Darkseid."

BADABING: "I am a stereotype."

Chapter 11

When the Carnage Happens

Now that you've worked out every angle to ensure that your campaign of mayhem will have its greatest possible impact and really communicate exactly what you want to say to the world, it's time to put yourself out there. Or don't put yourself out there, however you want to do it. What I mean is: It's time to start melting some things . . . like faces.

There are multiple ways to approach this:

- You may go in for the quick hit.
- You may stretch things out.
- You may place yourself right in the middle of the fray.
- You may remove yourself from it entirely.

Try to look badass around any and all explosions.

There's really no wrong way to go about it.* That said, you should choose a stratagem that is best suited to your skills and gimmickry.

Supervillain FAQ: What fight training do I need?

In a perfect world, we would all be able to build fortresses on the moon and make oceans boil peacefully and at our leisure. But it's not a perfect world, and, occasionally, people who see some sort of moral problem with our activities come into those fortresses—our private property—and try to do us harm. And, as much as we may want to slide our way out of legitimate fights by virtue of being slippery sons of bitches, sometimes you'll have no option but to put up your dukes.

So it is incumbent for those of us in the supervillain community to learn a few pugilistic tricks of our own; to stave off those attackers and protect our soft spots. But there are so many different fighting styles out there. What technique best suits the evil set?

Consider these questions:

---

* You should note that there are literally thousands of wrong ways to go about this.

Do you know magic?

If so, then use that shit. No punching can do more to terrify and harm than shooting fireballs at someone's face. Or turning someone into a frog. Or making their hands their feet.**

How big are you?

If you've got some size and strength, offensive moves, kicks and throws and the like are worth trying out. If you're smaller and wimpier in stature, think about defensive fighting; like the kind where you jump inside a giant, impenetrable metal ball and roll yourself away while screaming.

If you live in a video game, that helps.

** Bonus: This is also hilarious.

Who's your opponent?

Maybe you're going up against a hulking brawler. In that case, a more fluid, lithe style could serve as a contrast. Or maybe the person you're fighting has a lot of agility. Strength training and precision can bring them down with much force. If your nemesis is an ancient kung fu master, consider developing a fighting technique in which you drop to your knees and beg for mercy.

How hard are you willing to work to become a great fighter?

If your answer is "not very," as I'm sure it is for most of you, just hire some people who already know how to fight and have them stand around you at all times . . . even in when you're taking a dump.

Are you a fair fighter?

Of course you're not. Go for the junk.

Length of Attack
The Surgical Strike

Just because a statement is brief, doesn't mean it isn't powerful. If all you wish to do is swoop in, drain a septic tank into the DMV, and get out of there (more on how to get out of there shortly), that's your prerogative. I know I said last chapter that you should be playing the long game, and I still hold to that, but playing the long game doesn't always necessitate that every gambit include 1,000 moving pieces. A quick strike may be all you need to do at this juncture. You handle this in one devastating move, but just as long as it coincides with a larger scheme down the road. Not everything has to be a symphony. Sometimes a catchy pop song will suffice; especially if those pop songs pile up over the years. People may want to murder you for putting that earworm in their ears, but you'll already be gone . . . until you come back and do it again.

Making It Personal

Much of what I've discussed to this point aims more toward a general property damage and loss-of-life type of scenario, but just as effective is a plan of attack that looks to wear down one target—preferably your arch-nemesis—until everything that they have in the world is reduced to nothing; or driven so far away that the hero can no longer see it. Sure, the price tag will be smaller, but the damage you can do to one particularly difficult individual may make the disparity worth it. Consider this less a pop song than a ballad . . . a hate ballad.

A Prolonged Offensive

With that said, it does often feel more satisfying to really draw out your composition; to see the looks on the faces of your shocked audience as you not only drain the reservoir and flood the DMV, but also destroy all the cars in the city over a matter of weeks and revoke everyone's driver's licenses through a specialized computer virus. Imagine the chaos and helplessness people will experience during that lengthy offensive, worried about what will come next as you gracefully segue into your next movement. You should note, however, that there's a solid chance someone will locate you and try to pound you into jelly as your campaign progresses. If you want to avoid that very likely consequence, go for something faster.

WORST PRACTICE IN ACTION: Doc Ock Goes for the Ultimate Defense

Without even being aware of it, Doctor Octopus almost had the best possible defense; one that would have insulated him from Spider-Man's attacks for years: He nearly married Peter Parker's Aunt May. Sure, he was only doing it so he could get access to a secret island with a nuclear reactor on it, which Aunt May had inexplicably inherited for some reason. But Hammerhead ruined it all by busting in on the wedding, although it was a valiant effort while it lasted.

Teaching Moment: Randomly courting and/or marrying senior citizens could lead you toward conveniently marrying a parental figure of your arch-nemesis, which severely limits their options when it comes to dealing with you. Though it may seem you're blindly reaching for an unlikely coincidence, remember the Law of Coincidences. They're the rule.

Your Location

Leading the Charge

- Are you a rough-and-tumble brawler?
- Is your destructive plan entirely dependent on your superpowers, e.g., you're an electricity-based supervillain trying to overload the electrical system so no one can watch the newest *Homeland*, which means they'll all be an episode behind and extremely frustrated when they see everyone else talking about it online the next day?
- Do you feel a compulsion to be seen, and not just on screens all around the city, but in person?
- Do you have some sort of power that requires you to feed off the fear of people directly in front of you?
- Are you a centaur of some kind?
- Do you have a death wish?

These are all valid reasons for wishing to lead your henchmen into the fray. Otherwise, why in the hell would you want to do that?

Observing from Behind

Like the military generals of old, you could stay back along the edge of the battlefield and look on from your tent as the decimation plays out in front of you. You may say, "That's cowardly," but as I've stated before, what's so improper about being cowardly? You didn't get to this position just so you could go get stabbed with energy blades all afternoon. You have people to do that for you. Let them put on a show for you. Of course, you will need to be in constant contact with your henchman leader on the ground to ensure that they do everything correctly. I mean, you don't want them accidentally summoning the wrong demons, do you?

Taking a Bird's-Eye View

Same as observing from behind, but this you get to do from a blimp or a hot-air balloon. Communication may be a bit tougher, and there's always the chance of being shot down, but I'd say those risks are worth the fun.

Behind the Curtain

If I haven't already made this abundantly clear, theatrics play a big role in our lives as bad guys. So you may want to consider sending surrogates into the fray early on; even potentially obfuscating the notion that you're behind any of this until exactly the right dramatic moment in which you spring out from your hiding spot and reveal to your arch-nemesis and anyone else who might be around that, yes, it was indeed you who plan out this whole series of attacks aimed at snuffing out everything your targets hold dear. As such, this makes for an especially impactful moment when your focus is on a single individual's personal sanity and/or happiness.

Watching on Monitors from a Bunker

Again, cowardice is not actually a problem. Hunkering down in a secure bunker located forty stories under the earth's surface is a perfectly reasonable response to being a person responsible for replacing all the bricks in the city with ferrets.

Exit Strategies

As the famous supervillain, The Gambler (who managed to keep his identity secret under the guise of singer Kenny Rogers for decades), sang so succinctly, "you've got to know when to fold 'em." But once you're finished bending your enemies in half, you also have to know when to pull up stakes and get out of there before you're overwhelmed by the authorities' opposing forces. As I said in Chapter 2, it's always worthwhile to have an escape route. Here are a few specific methods to have at the ready:

- Helicopter with convenient rope ladder that comes straight to you
- Giant drill
- Teleportation device and/or powers

- Giant whale that swallows you and takes you elsewhere
- Turns out you were impressionist Rich Little all along
- Wildly flap your arms and see what happens
- Smoke pellets, hundreds of them
- Rocket pack and/or boots
- Pneumatic tubes (these takes some planning)
- Hire a band to "play you off"; according to decorum, no one can stop you
- Pick some rube to switch bodies with
- Have the artist who drew you erase you and draw you somewhere else
- Pay everyone off to just clam up about it.*

Dish It Out but Don't Take It: Avoiding Harm

We live in a world blindly and unnecessarily obsessed with the concept of fairness. When you roll into town and smash up a bunch of people's stuff (and also their organs), all of a sudden there will be all these other people—particularly the superpowered and caped ones; some of them monsters who are literally made out of rocks—who will want to similarly smash you up out of some sense of getting retribution or payback.

It's so unfair.

This is why you have to make every effort you can to protect yourself from the dangerous fists and

---

* More on this in the next chapter.

other offensive maneuvers of superheroic attackers. Consider the following defensive measures:

Wearing a Helmet

Yes, you might think these look dorky or cover up your lustrous hair, but let me tell you something. If it's good (bad) enough for Magneto, it's good (bad) enough for you.**

Use Decoys (again)

I discussed these in Chapter 2 as a way of throwing enemies off your scent. But what about when somebody is already on your scent? It doesn't matter if it's a hologram or a robot; anything that looks like you that isn't you and that can take a 10-megaton punch in your place is worth having.

Generate a Protective Force Field

Not only do they keep out punches, but they also look pretty damn cool if you're floating around in one that's got all sorts of crackling electrical energy surrounding it.

Smoke

Most heroes are avid, obnoxious non-smokers, who will throw themselves into a shockingly dramatic coughing fit the second they catch a whiff of

---

** And anyway, helmets can serve as a worthy substitute for hair. I said so myself back in Chapter 1, which means it must be true.

any second-hand smoke you blow their way. This can offer you a window of reprieve.

Body Armor
Won't do you a ton of good to fend off hand-to-hand assaults, which is the method most superheroes prefer, but you'll *feel* safer.

Surround Yourself with Other People
Not for camaraderie or human feeling; just so you can throw someone else to the wolves when they tear down your door.

Trap Doors
Try to only go places where you know that you have at least six to ten trap doors surrounding the spot where you're standing at any given time, and that you have access to those trap doors' latches.

Learn How to Increase or Decrease Your Size at Will
Punches won't mean much—even from the strongest heroes—if you're 1,000 feet tall. (Unless, of course, they are also that size. Best to check into that.) Likewise, being insanely tiny means they won't be able to find you in order to punch you. Either one could work.

Just Plain Be a Slippery Son of a Bitch
This will really be the thing that gets you out of more scrapes than anything else.

Chapter 12

Money

In *The Supervillain Handbook*, I briefly discussed how important financial planning is in the world of professional super-evil. And, quite obviously, I was fully justified in doing so. Properly managing your funds could mean the difference between leading your malevolent empire from a skyscraper you own and planning out a plot to hold up a Sonic while trying not to make too much noise in your uncle's garage.

Of course, there's more to supervillainous finances than acquiring funds and making sure you don't spend too much of it on stupid crap like bobble heads of yourself. (Incidentally, King Oblivion, Ph.D. bobble heads remain available at bargain basement prices.) How you display your affluence and/or avarice is a key component of building your reputation as a shining bastion of reckless professional evil. Don't spend your funds on one kind of stupid crap. Spend it on entirely different stupid crap.

Supervillain FAQ: So what if I die?

They say the only two sure things in life are death and taxes. Of course, most people pay their taxes once a year and only die once. As a supervillain, you'll do something in the area of the exact opposite (if you pay taxes, ever). Dying is something you have to expect and accept when you enter this business. You get used to it after a while. Because you always come back. Every time.

In case you don't believe me (and my monitoring of your thoughts indicates that some of you remain doubters *even now*, and you can rest assured some laser drones are coming to your home imminently), listen to this compelling testimony from Grieveless, the Woman Who Resurrects.

> Some of you guys, you're lucky. You only die maybe three, four times in your career. I die just about every week. It's my superpower. I have to do it.

> I know, it sounds like a weird gig. But I actually get a solid amount of work; jobbing for the bigger-name mastermind types, you know? They need to fool some caped jerk into thinking a lady got blasted with a cannon, I'm there. Human shield? That's me. Sometimes I step in to make it look like one of them got offed when it was really me in that plane crashing into a river of lava. It's why they never find a body.

> It pays pretty well. But that's not what you want to know, right? You want to know what it's like when the lights go out. Well. Don't say I didn't warn you.

So the first thing is that there's a lot of pain. Like, searing pain in the back of your eyeballs. The death itself, where you take it, may not even have anything to do with your eyeballs, but that's where you feel it. I guess 'cause that's where you really live your life, there in your head. Look, I'm not a biologist. I'm just telling you how it all feels.

Is this what you're lookin' for? Seems awfully morbid to talk about this kind of stuff, and I live it every day. Anyways . . .

The next thing is pure darkness for a while. Just black. I'd tell you how long it lasts, but it's sort of this feeling of there being no time. It's entirely black and there's no time. Until there is.

That's when you sort of wake up as this consciousness. No body, no real sense of space, just this thing in this place, and you may recognize other things in that place. Like, last time I was down there, I saw The Comptroller. Remember that guy? He was yelling some stuff about . . . you know, maybe it was you! What a weird coincidence, right? Anyway, it's stuffy in there. It's not hell. I've been to hell and they've got some great buffets there. This place is just some place where your consciousness gets jammed in with other consciousnesses, like some kid put you all in a mason jar.

And then, after a while, you come back to your body; at a morgue, or buried in a shallow grave, or still floating in a lake somewhere. If your body got all burned up or melted? You usually wake up in a garbage bin behind T.G.I. Friday's. Don't ask me to explain that one.

So that's about it on how things go when you die and come back. Is that all you needed? Can I go back to my apartment now? I was just finishing up a real cool watercolor of some dogs eating at a diner like they're people. You really got to see it; it's a hoot and a half—

Oh, so I guess you've already decided to crush me with these spikes then. Well, okay then. It's been a swell time. See you around, King.

For the record, that painting was trash.

Let me put it to you as a rhetorical question, because that's the way I most like to convey things: What's the point of stealing, counterfeiting, scamming, printing, conjuring, inheriting, or, ugh, as much as I hate to include it, earning money if you can't flaunt it?

There isn't one.

Go big. Every time.

To pose another rhetorical question: What's more evil than using money that could go toward helping others for entirely frivolous displays of status? Again: Not a thing. So put that paper to bad use in one of the following ways:

Build an Impossible Lair

In my previous book, I listed the various types of lairs one might consider. But really, that choice is all about personal preference and comfort. If you want a lair that really goads your evil rep, what you absolutely need is something that is basically impossible:

- An ice palace in the center of the Earth;
- A space fortress with bay windows you can open;
- An underwater lab made out of fish food.

Whatever it is, make it incredibly huge and insanely impractical. The more you spend on this confounding artifact, the more astonished anyone who meets you will be.

Obtain Precious Material-Related Scars and Injuries

While this is more the purview of James Bond-style spy villains rather than superhero-fighting supervillains, it's a worthy page to steal from their playbook. Some diamonds embedded in your left eye socket, a giant scar down your arm made out of platinum, or a colostomy bag full of Cristal Champagne lets everyone know that you don't just buy the most expensive stuff. You *are* the most expensive stuff.

Buy More Vehicles than You Can Possibly Use

In Chapter 3, I listed the numerous options you have when it comes to getting around town and told you to pick the one that best suits you. But here's a little secret: If you have enough power and money, you can travel in all those ways . . . and more. Make your lair its own vehicle. Pay some people to let you ride around on them like horses (or worse yet, don't pay them). Buy a helicopter. Then buy a jumbo jet *for your helicopter*. Then put those in a blimp. Make a turducken of vehicles. Then crash them whenever you feel like it. People who can barely afford the payments on their 1997 Honda Civic will despise and fear you in ways you can't even imagine.

Wear a New Pair of Socks Every Day

There's nothing particularly evil about doing this, other than the wastefulness (I advise you to burn each pair as soon as you take them off to ensure no one else can be blessed by wearing socks that have adorned your almighty feet), but wouldn't it just be the coolest thing ever to wear new socks every day? Let me tell you: It is.

Start or Invest in Legitimate Businesses

One of the ways to really cheese off people who have nothing is to do that thing all rich people do: Earn money by having money. So shove your privilege in their faces by dumping loads of cash into businesses and reaping the reward of their profits. Of course, the one downside to this is that most businesses would prefer to keep their distance from outright evil causes, since the consumers who buy their products aren't always totally into that stuff. That's why you've got to make sure to brand everything you get involved in so that it has a sheen of "goodness," or whatever that is. Consider these examples next time you want to christen a business and make it more palatable to the masses:

- Non-Murderous Chemical Inc.
- Poison-Free Burger Hut
- Smiley Fun Blade Knife Manufacture
- Illicit Drugs Are Bad Ice Cream Delivery Service
- DeAnimated Mortuary, L.L.C.

- It Was Like That When We Got Here Security Concern
- Body-Sized Bags of Love Waste Management Co.
- We Give a Shit About Our Employees Mega-Mart
- Honest Honest Honest Honest Honest Honest Media
- What Kind of Dog and Pony Show Do You Think This Is? Look At Our Books If You Want Proof Accounting
- Altria Group
- Wholesome, and Delicious Candy, You Know, For Kids Worldwide

What shouldn't you name your company? "Beats by Dre." Who would want to take a beating from Dr. Dre; especially since that guy got all ripped? That's just terrible marketing.

Start or Invest in Illegitimate Businesses

If you're not so worried about whether you earn any money back from your business ventures, go in full force with evil intent:

- Start a company that makes Draculas, or find someone whose company mission statement is to burn up most of the world's oil and hoard all the rest.
- Give that person or company an insanely large amount of money.
- Provide seed funding to a startup in another dimension where someone is breeding Murder Bugs.
- Fund experiments that replace peoples' arms and legs with farm animals.
- See if you can build a giant working mouth in the middle of the Gobi Desert.

- Buy a bunch of Goldman Sachs stock.
- Fund Uwe Boll movies.

The more nefarious the intent, the better (worse).

Found a "Charity"

The badly kept secret about charities is that people donate to them not so much because they want to actually do things for other people, but to keep themselves from feeling guilty for living the charmed life. So give them something to funnel their money into. Start a 'Caring Society for the Victims of Death Ray Blastings'; open up the coffers and start collecting funds. Then plow those funds back into your gala events and fundraisers. The more events you have, the more people out there will know that you're a financial force to be reckoned with. No one will know where the money's really going, nor will they care. And the real trick is that, as you're holding more events, you'll be creating scads of new death ray victims every week for people to feel guilty about. It's a damn near perfect scheme.

WORST PRACTICE IN ACTION: Ra's al Ghul Makes It Rain

For a 700-year-old, Ra's al Ghul certainly knows how to spend his cash. He uses his funds not only for regular eco-terrorism—he gained much of his wealth by killing a king with contaminated fabrics—but for the upkeep of the "Lazarus pits" that keep him basically immortal and to run a criminal organization that is called, with no irony whatsoever, The Demon.

Teaching Moment: It's hard to think of a cooler way to spend one's money than creating giant organizations with names like "The Demon," and maintaining immortality pits. Just saying.

Other "Largesse"

You could actually give money to people who need it, but only if they come to your big event in the city's central square where monsters come out of the sewers and drag them into them. You ask me, I think that's a pretty fair trade.

Start a Ponzi and/or Pyramid Scheme

If starting up an organization that's nominally supposed to do good in the world makes you feel conflicted, that is, if you want to do nothing but unadulterated evil, then go ahead and boldfacedly swindle people. There's no harm in that, except for the immense harm you'll be doing to everyone involved.

Throw Extravagant Parties

Again, if charity isn't a direction in which you want to go, you can at least have some big bashes. Fill a pool with champagne and invite people to swim in it. Have one of those parties where people bring losers and everyone laughs at them. Have an orgy. Whatever you want to do, just make sure that tons of people are invited and everyone knows about how much scrilla (that's what the kids call money these days) you're throwing around. Then, when it's all over, shake everyone down for "donations" to fill your own pockets.*

Fund Important Research

Of course, by "important," what I really mean is you should dump a bunch of money into paying idiot scientists to figure out a way to finally wipe your moron superhero nemesis off the planet. They'll probably never do it because, if your genius isn't enough to pull it off, how could theirs be? But you have to keep trying.

Bribe Elected Officials

It's always handy to have some corrupt people in power in your pocket to help you slip the noose during trials or just walk out of jail on technicalities or unfair charges. Plus,

---

* This is a subtle way of saying you should rob them.

whenever you turn on those officials and tell them that you're taking over their city, they'll be nothing but pawns of yours. And if they're lucky, they'll be so hilariously shocked. It's a hoot to see.

Eat Increasingly Crazy and Expensive Food

Caviar? Pssh. Wagyu beef? Come on. Snark fin soup? Pedestrian. You've got to find the really, insanely expensive stuff to dine on. Like, maybe a casserole made with broccoli, cheese, and Mark Twain's original hand-written notes for *Huckleberry Finn*. How good would a pizza topped with the Betsy Ross's original American flag be? What about a milkshake infused with Napoleon's remains? Maybe you knock down the Parthenon, grind it into dust, and eat that? Sanity be damned, you're hungry!

Buy a Bunch of Bobble Heads of Me

I know I said earlier you shouldn't waste your money on bobble heads of yourself, but that's only because there are so many of me available and those are better. So buy those. *Buy them, you stingy dirtbags.*

Simply Destroy All Money

If what you want to do is incite anger and raw jealously immediately, consider throwing all your money (which was quite recently everyone else's money) into a river somewhere. That will definitely do the trick.

Waste All, Want All: Protecting Your Assets

I'm encouraging you to waste your money; but that doesn't mean it should go unsecured. Those dollars (or pounds, or EvilBucks, or whatever they may be) are yours to waste as you please. They're not for some rabble-rousers or superheroes or, worse, other supervillains, to sneak up and skulk away with under your very nose. It requires proactive measures to ensure your holdings remain yours until such time as you fritter it away or destroy it. One or all of these measures will keep your money and other liquid assets safe until you use it for the devilish purpose of your choice:

Hire Armed Guards
A little run-of-the-mill, I know, but when you have a literal army of guys who dress similarly to the way you do, why not post them outside the various storehouses where you keep your stuff? What else are they going to do, spend time with their families and sleep?

Keep Your Accounts Offshore
For many rich businesspeople, this means putting your money in secret accounts in small island nations or that national fortress of "we won't tell if you don't," Switzerland. For supervillains, it means piling all your cash, treasure, and other valuables into a submarine and tossing it into the ocean so no one else can get it.

Bury It

If dumping all your money into the ocean seems a bit extreme, take a cue from some of the earliest proto-supervillains: pirates. Dig a big hole in some woods or in a cave and put all your stuff down in there. If you create a map to locate your stuff later, you should probably just come to terms with the fact that some dashing swashbuckler is going to try to steal that map at some point in the future. To keep that from happening, bury your map.*

Build a Money Bin

Scrooge McDuck may have nominally been a hero—though he did defeat the Beagle Boys one too many times for my liking—but he was also a renowned penny pincher who kept all his money in coin form, piled high enough so he could swim in it, in a giant building with a dollar sign on it. If that's not super-villain-style behavior, I don't know what is.**

Wear It

If you or a close tailor friend of yours (who you'll have to kill afterward, just FYI) design a suit of money for you to wear, you'll never have to worry about your cash ever leaving your sight. That is, if you resign yourself to never taking your clothes

---

* Make sure to mark an X over your buried map, then cover the X with dirt, so that no one finds it.

** I do know what is. I wrote the book on it. Two books on it! My point is: Never doubt me again.

off. I guess you'll have to experience some uncomfortable visits to the gym and get very little sleep. You could also invest your bills into precious metals or jewels and have someone make clothing out of that for you. A ruby jumpsuit would be cool. Or you could get a sculptor to mold a solid-platinum facemask for you so you can finally one-up that show-off Destro.

Send it Back in Time
A bunch of wooly mammoths or Cro-Magnon people aren't going to give two shits about some piles

of green paper adorned with the faces of people who won't be born for millennia.

Though you should be cautious to avoid fault lines and volcanoes.

And places where meteors could land.

And anywhere near an area where animals that might eat leaf-like paper would likely be roaming around. Maybe you should build that money bin back in 300,000 BCE, as well.

Epilogue

Leaving the Stage

This manual has offered many useful and proven tips for making your career in supervillainy a long and accomplished one, but even the most evil and/or immortal of us have to let go of the reins and step away at some point. Everything comes to an end. For some supervillains, that end may come after centuries of work in the field of organized chaos. For others, it may come sooner than they think.

For you, the end comes *right now*.

Listen. Why in this universe or any other would I, the leading supervillain the profession, want to go about creating thousands upon thousands of upstart evil doers to usurp me down the line? That would be madness. It would be against my very interests. And though I'm altogether insane, I'm not a masochist. Did you not read what I did to the individual supervillains I pumped for anecdotes throughout this text? How did you think you'd come out of this any differently? Plus, I stole your thoughts at the end of the last book. You'd think you'd learn. You'd think.

All I needed was a window of your attention, so I could creep into your minds and seize your neurons.

In the time it's taken for you to thumb through these pages, inform yourself, look at some colorful illustrations, have a few laughs (I don't know why but some people have told me these books were "funny" prior to my shoving them into a furnace), I've been using my improved Psychomonitor, which I have rechristened as the Cortex Controller, to not only collect your thoughts throughout, but also to slowly take charge of your motor functions.

You should know this already. I told you I was going to do it 200 or so pages ago. You thought just because I *said* I was joking, that I really was? You all deserve your fate, then. You should know full well that any joke a supervillain tells is the truth wrapped in a lie wrapped in further lies and truths. You should trust everything I say, as well as not trust it.

It seems you have learned nothing. Perhaps this is the way things should have happened anyway.

With this book, I have taken over your bodies, in addition to your minds. Now you are nothing but putty in my hands to be molded and shaped as I please. Not to say that you weren't already under my power to a degree already; after all, you spent a modest portion of your money on this guide which you had to at least have an inkling might be a grand trick to take control of your every movement. You had to be at least somewhat aware of it, right? Are you all really that gullible?

No matter.

I believe my first act as your puppet master will be to send you to the nearest bookstore so you can buy a dozen, two dozen, or three dozen more copies of this guide. Then you will come to me, to serve out your time as perhaps a henchman or a footstool or a footstool for one of my footstools.

This will be your new life. Not as a supervillain, but as chattel. As a servant of the greatest supervillain to ever grace existence.

You're welcome.

Those of you who read from the beginning know full well that none of this exercise had any real meaning; I have cut your legs out from under you. You are powerless. What use do you have now for knowledge of controlling the media, something I am now free to do alone?

But some readers—rule-breakers by nature—have an inclination to flip to the end and discover the ending before they begin. And, really, can I blame them? They wish to be supervillains. I can't really discourage them from deviating from the mores of book-reading culture.

To avoid spoiling the surprise of their utter defeat, the following pages provide them with a glossary of supervillain terms that media professionals also use. They'll think that information has some use to them. You'll know it's nothing but a mildly amusing distraction as you continue your meaningless existence.

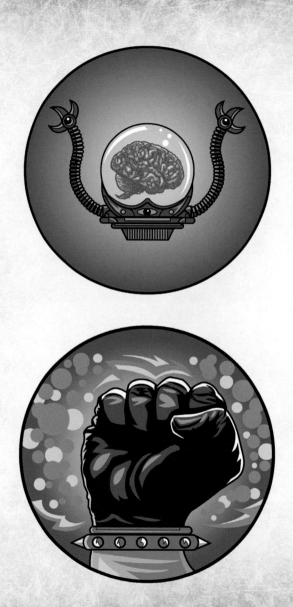

Appendix

The Supervillain vs. Media Glossary

Y ou may have been somewhat surprised to discover, through this guide, just how important the news media is for supervillains looking to cement a reputation for evil so prevalent that it becomes a part of people's day-to-day lives and thoughts. The media isn't merely important; it's necessary to any sort of mass messaging: The kind of messaging one must perform to reach the heights of super-evil.

And as much as we supervillains may find it more convenient to simply take over the satellites at the nearest broadcast station, we occasionally find that cooperation with the media of one kind or another is the only real course. Before one versed in the ways of professional calamity interacts with the media community, however, one should make themselves aware of the terminology villainy shares with the journalistic profession. It's a surprisingly long list of terms, and mistake a request for a media-specific favor for something nefariousness-related could lose you a great deal of precious, precious publicity. Be mindful of these double meanings and get airtime rather than jail time.

anchor

   <u>What it means to them</u>: A television or radio personality who presents the news.

   <u>What it means to you</u>: What you tie to the victims of the deep-sea Weresharks you've been breeding.

angle

   <u>What it means to them</u>: The aspect of a story a reporter chooses to highlight.

   <u>What it means to you</u>: The term for the positioning of your giant fly-swatter to ensure you hit Moe Squito when he tries to attack your lair.

attribute

   <u>What it means to them</u>: To give the proper identification of a speaker.

   <u>What it means to you</u>: Something you never do for anyone else when it comes to credit, and do for everyone else when it comes to blame.

banner

   <u>What it means to them</u>: The large headline at the top of a page.

   <u>What it means to you</u>: That guy who turns into that big green thing you run away from.

beat

   <u>What it means to them</u>: A subject a reporter regularly covers.

   <u>What it means to you</u>: How you get your henchmen to listen.

blind

   <u>What it means to them</u>: Term describing a source which is not named.

What it means to you: What you do to someone who refuses to penitently say your name.

breaking

What it means to them: Happening right now.

What it means to you: What may be happening to your bones right now if a bullying superhero is around.

circulation

What it means to them: The number of copies or issues a print publication distributes.

What it means to you: The machine you're developing to cut off in everyone's hands and feet, creating an epidemic of cold extremities throughout the city so that they mayor will acquiesce to your demands.

clip

What it means to them: A short piece of audio or video.

What it means to you: What you're going to do to any pedestrian superheroes next time you're out driving.

column

What it means to them: An opinion article written by a credited author.

What it means to you: What Pliny the Immortal hit you with last month and are still smarting from.

dead air

What it means to them: A portion of a broadcast with no content.

What it means to you: The result of your short-lived war against air.

double truck

What it means to them: A two-page spread of content.

<u>What it means to you</u>: What the Burt Reynolds impersonator crime duo, The Bandits, drive.

edit

<u>What it means to them</u>: To revise, correct, and/or shorten.

<u>What it means to you</u>: Basically just to shorten; usually at the legs.

embargo

<u>What it means to them</u>: To hold a story until a particular date.

<u>What it means to you</u>: What every other nation does to yours when you declare a sovereign state.

fact

<u>What it means to them</u>: A verifiable piece of information.

<u>What it means to you</u>: Your brilliance, and very little else.

feedback

<u>What it means to them</u>: A sound generated when a microphone is improperly calibrated.

<u>What it means to you</u>: The result of your experiments sewing mouths on to the spines of henchmen.

gutter

<u>What it means to them</u>: The vertical margin between two pages.

<u>What it means to you</u>: The place you find henchmen.

headline

<u>What it means to them</u>: A short bit of text describing the contents of an article.

<u>What it means to you</u>: The mark on some supervillains' skulls that results from repeated superpowered punching to the cranium.

human interest

<u>What it means to them</u>: An often-emotional story about non-famous people.

<u>What it means to you</u>: What you feel occasionally, but only in terms of what people might look like as ferrets.

interview

<u>What it means to them</u>: A conversation for broadcast or publication.

<u>What it means to you</u>: What you see when you shrink down and go inside someone's body.

kicker

<u>What it means to them</u>: The last line of an article.

<u>What it means to you</u>: That guy you hired to go around and kick people for you.

lead

<u>What it means to them</u>: The first line of an article.

<u>What it means to you</u>: What you will do to any reporter you speak to, as well as everyone else, eventually.

libel

<u>What it means to them</u>: To print false and defamatory information about someone.

<u>What it means to you</u>: General conversation. (see slander)

mug shot

<u>What it means to them</u>: A close-up photo of someone's face.*

<u>What it means to you</u>: What you take at the vessel your superhero nemesis' uses for morning coffee, just to annoy them.

---

* Alternately, also a picture taken of someone after an arrest.

off-the-record

    <u>What it means to them</u>: Not for publication.

    <u>What it means to you</u>: What happens when that insanely lucky superhero somehow removes their bindings and escapes the giant turntable before going under the huge, razor-sharp needle.

plagiarize

    <u>What it means to them</u>: To use another's work as your own.

    <u>What it means to you</u>: Writing; an offense punishable by death (applicable to me only)

Q & A

    <u>What it means to them</u>: An article presented as questions and answers.

    <u>What it means to you</u>: Quit and Abscond, the pillars of cowardice, also known as the supervillain's standard escape plan.

release

    <u>What it means to them</u>: A public relations document informing reporters of news.

    <u>What it means to you</u>: What you never do to prisoners, ever.

retract

    <u>What it means to them</u>: To pull a story back after it is proven false or misleading.

    <u>What it means to you</u>: What you want the mechanical claws welded to your torso to be capable of doing, so you can go out in public without having to explain yourself every few steps.

sic

What it means to them: Indicates an already-existing grammatical error in quoted text.

What it means to you: What the lion-hounds do.

shoot

What it means to them: Take a photograph or video.

What it means to you: What your ray guns do.

stand-up

What it means to them: A piece of footage in which a television reporter stands in front of a camera and relates the details of a story.

What it means to you: What you can't do for most of the week after a superhero fight.

thumbnail

What it means to them: A small version of a photo, for archiving.

What it means to you: A particularly effective place to stick a piece of bamboo.

two-shot

What it means to them: A video frame in which two people can be seen.

What it means to you: What two ray guns do.

wire service

What it means to them: An organization which sends out syndicated news articles.

What it means to you: Your hire that's great with garroting.

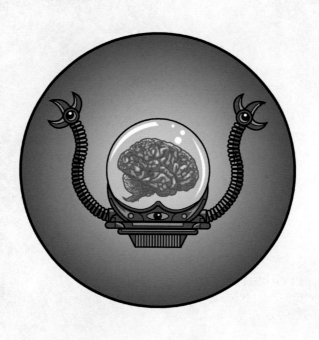

ALSO AVAILABLE

"Without great supervillains, superheroes would have no one to fight but each other! King Oblivion, Ph.D., has performed a noble public service with *The Supervillain Handbook* and deserves the unbounded gratitude of every thinking comic book fan. Excelsior!" —STAN LEE

THE SUPERVILLAIN HANDBOOK
The Ultimate How-to Guide to Destruction and Mayhem

KING OBLIVION, PH.D.
(as told to Matt D. Wilson)
Illustrated by Adam Wallenta

The Supervillain Handbook
by King Oblivion, Ph.D., as told to Matt D. Wilson
Illustrated by Adam Wallenta

Looking for a way out of the rat race? Tired of your ho-hum, workaday life? Have an inexplicable love of turning human beings into inanimate objects? Then professional supervillainy might just be for you! With tips from the renowned founder and overlord of the International Society of Supervillains, *The Supervillain Handbook* is your one-stop-shop for everything evil. Gain invaluable insight on the art of revenge, choosing your evil name, where to find the perfect lair, and much more!

$12.95 Paperback • ISBN 978-1-61608-711-1

Yeah, that's right, I'm so evil that I'm plugging my book twice!

ALSO AVAILABLE

The Supervillain Handbook
by King Oblivion, Ph.D., as told to Matt D. Wilson
Illustrated by Adam Wallenta

Looking for a way out of the rat race? Tired of your ho-hum, workaday life? Have an inexplicable love of turning human beings into inanimate objects? Then professional supervillainy might just be for you! With tips from the renowned founder and overlord of the International Society of Supervillains, *The Supervillain Handbook* is your one-stop-shop for everything evil. Gain invaluable insight on the art of revenge, choosing your evil name, where to find the perfect lair, and much more!